Murder in
the Marsh

Kevin Carey

www.darkstroke.com

Discover us online:
www.darkstroke.com

Join us on instagram:
www.instagram.com/darkstrokebooks/

Include **#darkstroke** in a photo of yourself
holding this book on Instagram and
something nice will happen.

*For Bill Z and Walter
and the FDU MFA crew*

Acknowledgements

I'd like to thank the people who first read this novel in its various stages, Jack Herzog, Tim Young, Bill Barton, Jim DeFilippi, and my life-long friend, Ed Boyle, and the good folks at Salem Writers Group for listening to excerpts over time. Thanks to the poets, RG Evans, Jennifer Martelli and January O'Neil for the epigraphs. And a special thanks to my kids, Kevin and Michaela, you always inspire me, and to my wife Betty, who is always in my corner.

Having grown up in Revere, Massachusetts, I want to thank the people of Revere for their goodwill and friendship over the years. The people and the situations in this novel are made entirely of fiction. Any resemblance to actual people or events is purely coincidental.

Lastly, if you or a loved one are victims of abuse or sexual violence (or feel threatened) please know there is help out there. Call The National Domestic Violence hotline at 1-800-799-7233, 1-800-787-3224 TTY, or text 'LOVEIS' to 1-866-331-9474, or chat online at thehotline.org

About the Author

Kevin Carey is the author of three collections of poetry from CavanKerry Press, *The One Fifteen to Penn Station, Jesus Was a Homeboy*, which was selected as an Honor Book for the 2017 Paterson Poetry Prize, and the recently released *Set in Stone*, and a chapbook of fiction, *The Beach People* (Red Bird Chapbooks). He is also a filmmaker and playwright. His latest stage play "The Stand or Sal is Dead," a murder mystery comedy, premiered in Newburyport, MA. at The Actor's Studio in June of 2018.

More at: Kevincareywriter.com

Murder in
the Marsh

"A man believes that he is not a beast—
but really [he is] a snake who swallows
[his] own tail, all that's left:
the hunger and a pile of spoiled bodies
with no hearts left among them."

—RG Evans

Prologue
Summer 1980

Eddie Devlin spread the coarse, tall weeds in front of him like a curtain, the heavy rain driving him further into the dark marsh. When a shadow moved, he heard a mumbling through the wind. Sparks ran up his spine and a rush of blood filled his ears. He stepped forward on the rain-soaked turf— a flash of red in the darkness, a tall man standing in a flannel shirt, his face mostly hidden under his long, wet hair. *Was he laughing?*

Squinting through the rain, Eddie felt a twinge of recognition, *a dream maybe, a mug shot?* In that moment, he saw the bloody hooked blade in the man's hand and reached for his gun. The man fell forward to his knees, plunging the knife and ripping. Only then did Eddie see the girl, her body, her feet, her toenails painted red, and he yelled, "Drop the fucking knife." But he was already pulling the trigger, walking forward, firing a second time into the man's red-checkered chest, firing again and again, until the chamber of his gun clicked empty.

Part One - Cronus

"My Quarrel is this ancient blood within myself."

—Jennifer Martelli

Chapter One
Summer - 1981

Just outside of Boston, in the city of Revere, a three-mile, two-lane highway split the thousand acres of Rumney Marsh in two. The road, lined with tall cattails and switch grass, passed by a junkyard tucked into the wild weeds and on the north end, the tiny neighborhood of Oak Island. Sometimes the kids raced cars on the road in the summer, yelling into the marsh, but it was mostly a quiet, desolate stretch, only meant to get you to and from the beach as quickly as possible.

Eddie Devlin pulled his car over not far from Oak Island just as the sun was rising. He walked into the marsh alone, white high-cut sneakers, faded jeans, and a gray Celtics tee shirt he bought last spring after their fourteenth title — *1981 NBA Champs*. He was tall and a little hunched, his curly brown hair, flecked with gray now since he turned forty a few years ago, was moist from the humidity.

The swamp in front of him ran off to Route One, cars coming and going in all four lanes. At his back, across more marshland, pockets of two-story buildings and flat roof restaurants lined the three-mile beach boulevard in the shadow of the Boston Skyline.

This place always reminded Eddie of a *Creature Feature* that the movie house used to run on Saturday afternoons on Broadway when he was a kid. It might have begun with a quiet nature scene, the white egrets in ankle-deep puddles feasting on a fly-filled sandbar, but before long the beast hiding beneath the muddy water would find his way to the surface, and even though you knew what was coming, it still scared the shit out of you.

Looking at the sway of yellow swamp grass, he imagined

the bodies slipping along the mud floor beneath him— wise guys gone straight, gamblers, poor slobs who got too desperate or too stupid and ended up trunk cargo. They almost always got dumped into the marsh. Word around Revere Beach was that this place had enough body parts to make a football team of Frankenstein monsters. At one time Eddie thought that was funny, Frankenstein monsters playing football.

But, like all the other mornings he came here, he thought about the murder a year ago and the curse he had inherited. His mother used to say, "You're always in the shit, Eddie." She'd laugh and crush her cigarette into a big glass bowl of crooked dead butts.

She died three weeks after he got his patrolman stripes. "Someday you'll be sorry," she said on her deathbed, "chasing scum with a gun for a living."

Chapter Two

The rain drizzled on the windshield as Eddie pulled down the dead-end street and parked alongside the red-shingled box of a barroom, *Dana's Place*. The air was heavy, gearing up for another downpour that had made the marsh and the rest of the city a soaked sponge lately.

Inside, under low lights and the glare of a television set, three-hundred-pound Dana Costello leaned over the square bar and pointed to an open page from a racing book he had spread out before him. His brown suitcoat sleeve rose to his elbow. A young kid, maybe twenty-five, with a crew cut, looked on from the other side of the bar like he was reading a treasure map.

"Trust me," Dana said. "The three's a pig. If he don't run out of the one hole, forget him."

"Trust him, then ask me," Eddie said, reaching over the bar and grabbing a bottle of beer off the ice, looking the kid in the eyes. "He picked the Germans to win the Big One."

The kid wasn't sure if he should laugh or not.

"The Inspector returns," Dana said, walking over, the collar of his open white shirt stained a bit yellow around the neck.

"Just a memory soon."

"Today's the day?" Dana asked.

Eddie took a big swig of his beer, holding the tall neck with two fingers. "I can't wait."

"Fuck you. You're going to miss it."

"Time me," Eddie said.

Dana elbowed the bar in front of him. "You look like shit. You want the cot?"

Eddie did a quick scan of the place, the red padded booths

11

along the wall, the neon lines of the jukebox, a gray-haired guy in a crumpled tan suit talking to himself at the end of the bar. He could use it. Last night after the races, he sat in the track parking lot drinking himself sober with half-pint bottles of vodka, then let his green Grand Marquis find its way to the marsh, then the all-night donut shop on Shirley Ave for three large black coffees, then here.

Dana kept a roll-away in a small office— four wood-paneled walls with no windows, a desk, and a purple shag carpet from the sixties with a well-worn groove up the center. Eddie flipped the cot open and grabbed a pillow from the closet by the entrance. An electric fan built into the wall hummed to life. It relaxed him, that, and the fact that he knew Dana had his back and would dust him off if he woke up with the booze fits again.

Since the early days, they had been track buddies when Dana bought the bar and ran a little book out of the back room. Eddie turned the other way and got the other cops to look away with him, and the boys all drank on the cheap after hours. Eventually it got back to the brass and they had to find new soil to water, but Eddie never left, even if he had to pay for drinks, which was hardly ever.

He lay there on the cot imagining the speech Lieutenant Preston would give him later today, his deep voice, his own long sad story— the All-American tackle, the crackback block, and the Rose Bowl dreams up in smoke.

The whir of the fan blades went to work on him and before long the nightmare came calling, like it did every time he tried to sleep.

After he'd shot the attacker that night, almost a year ago to the day, he'd carried the girl to the road and covered her with a blanket from his car, whispering, "It's okay, it's over," the heavy rain driving into his bones.

When the uniforms showed up, he pointed them back into the marsh, but the attacker's body was gone. A short trail of blood ran into the swamp, but it could have been from the girl. The water rose quickly with each new downpour, and soon there was nothing, no trace, even after the helicopter and the floodlights and three days later, the futile attempt with a backhoe, nothing.

And then came the questions, the ones only Eddie could answer, and everyone from the brass to his buddies was asking them.

Why were you there? *I was heading home. I saw a car pulled over with a flat.*

Why did you walk into the marsh? *When I got out, I heard a sound. I followed it.*

Off duty, right? Were you drunk? *I'd had a few.*

When it was determined the wounds of the victim had been made with a curved blade, some reporter named the attacker *Cronus,* the Greek God often pictured with a sickle, who was said to have been banished beneath the dwelling of the human dead. After a while, it morphed into a reference for the incident and for Eddie himself, like Frankenstein for the name of the monster.

Chapter Three

Eddie had just finished brushing his teeth in the closet-sized john attached to the office when Dana pushed the door open and set a cup of coffee on the desk. "Thought you could use this."

"You're like a good old dog, D," Eddie said and put the toothbrush into a plastic bag he kept in the medicine cabinet.

"Never know when I'll need a cop."

A few minutes later, Eddie stepped into the open doorway of the barroom and leaned against the doorframe, the sidewalk slick and shaded in front of him. A fresh curtain of rain rolled in, followed by a distant burst of thunder. Teenagers hung on the sagging porch of a three-family across the street, drinking from cans and plastic cups. Eddie could smell the reefer floating down with the thick bass beats of a Disco song he hated.

Further down North Shore road he saw an old man in jeans and a long sleeve shirt waving a twelve-inch wooden cross to the passing traffic. "Repent," the man yelled. "Jesus is coming."

"Jesus is a homeboy," Eddie whispered.

The thunder got closer and the sky opened up, but the old man walked undaunted, screaming "Jesus saves" over the cracking sound and the pelting rain, looking wet and apocalyptic. A guy in a pickup truck honked and gave him the finger. The man made the sign of the cross and kept on. Eddie had seen him before, always with the sermon. He was a few yards away from the bar when he turned and yelled again, "Repent."

Eddie sipped his coffee and stared back. "Have a drink," he said.

"It's coming," the man replied. "The acid rain. You'll be left behind."

I'll take my chances, Eddie thought.

He watched the man head toward the boulevard where the beach people sat in their cars smoking cigarettes and drinking coffee, thinking about tans and getting laid and which scams to avoid or which ones to invent. People were generally confused these days, Eddie figured. It was the 80s; disco was hanging on, rock and roll was making a comeback, there was double-digit inflation, record unemployment, and divorce rates were up. People flocked to the dark all-night bar rooms and the afternoon happy hours in this town, while the government declared a war on drugs.

Dana snapped him out of it and put a big hand on his shoulder. "What now inspector? The pups might not run in this."

"Nothing, I guess," Eddie said and looked at him. "I feel like I've been doing nothing for a year, waiting to do more of nothing."

"Want a job here? Bouncer, bartender, whatever you want."

Eddie smiled. "I'm forty-three years old. Who am I going to bounce?" he said. "Besides, if I didn't pay for it once in a while, it would drive you shit house."

"I suppose," Dana said and looked down the road. "Maybe that preacher needs a helper."

"I could do that," Eddie said.

"If God didn't strike you down for fucking with him." Dana laughed.

Some joke, Eddie thought.

"Think of it this way," Dana said. "You can start over for the last time, right?"

"That's what sucks," Eddie said. "Whoever it was that cut that girl up a year ago…" He lit a cigarette. "Whoever it was could be sucking Cuban cigars on Miami Beach for all I know."

"Odds are he's worm bait under that marsh somewhere with a few rounds in his chest," Dana said and walked back inside, away from the rain, like a bear to his cave.

"Some odds," Eddie whispered, watching the smoke curl into the gray, wet sky like a dream.

Chapter Four
The Beast

One summer night, a year before Rumney Marsh got famous for the 1980 Cronus murder of Michelle Letti, and a year before Eddie Devlin found himself on probation for messing up a murder scene, Kyle Hardy and his only friend, John Allen, took the new girl from Maine out to see Dizzy bridge. "Gina with the big tits," they called her behind her back. She was fifteen and her father worked the dog track, which meant she was alone five nights a week.

They weren't the first Oak Island kids who tramped out to the small trestle bridge that supported the commuter train in and out of Boston. Many of them used it for fishing or jumping into the saltwater river on the hottest nights. The kids were wary of the train coming in fast but no strangers to it. They might lay a penny on the track or play chicken with a six-car commuter.

A story had gotten around that Kyle Hardy once tied a missing dog to the track, watched while it separated under the steaming wheel.

No one doubted it. Some of the boys grew strange out here. Most folks blamed it on the power lines that ran through the marsh; some said it was the isolation made them that way.

This night, a year before the Cronus murderer disappeared in the rain-soaked marsh, Kyle, John, and Gina were on their way back to Kyle's yard after drinking two bottles of wine he'd stolen from his father's cellar. They saw a horseshoe crab sneaking into the muddy river through the tall grass. Kyle, who stood above them in his cowboy boots and a sleeveless jean jacket, threw one of the empty bottles at it. "Fucking monster," he said. A train passed behind them, kicking dust off the tracks into the summer moonlight.

In the yard, they sat on benches by a brown picnic table and Kyle lit a joint and passed it across to Gina. She flicked some fallen ash off the front of her yellow halter top.

John Allen reached for the joint, then jumped up and ran to the bushes by Kyle's one car driveway. He heaved twice, then stood there for a few seconds with his hands on his knees. "I'm going home," he said and stumbled down the driveway to Oak Island Street. Kyle yelled, "Go on, wimp," just as Allen turned the corner out of sight.

Gina and Kyle passed the joint back and forth in silence. At one point Kyle got up and sat next to her. Gina was short, and Kyle had to lean down to kiss her. She didn't seem to mind, and she kissed him back. He smiled at her, his hair hanging in his face, so only one eye looked out. "Full moon," he said. "Could be a werewolf tonight." He kicked his head back and howled.

Gina laughed and looked at the moon herself. "What do think is up there?" she asked.

"I know it ain't made of cheese. I know that."

Kyle kissed her again, longer this time, and reached for her breast. She let him do it. But when he tried to put his hand down her pants, she pushed him away and stood up.

Kyle stood up too. "You're not turning shy on me, are you?"

"I gotta go," she said and stepped to his side, but he blocked her way, like a basketball player shuffling his feet on defense.

She stopped, more exasperated than scared. "I'm going home now, Kyle."

"Only when I say so," he said. "Remember, I'm the werewolf." He howled, which made her laugh a little, and she tried again to move past him.

"No, no," he said. "Not till I say so."

"And when is that?" she asked, swaying slightly back and forth.

Kyle stopped smiling and let his hand fall to the zipper of his pants. "When you're done." He reached to take himself

18

out and she kicked him between the legs, hard and only once. Kyle bent over and went to one knee and she walked around him. She could hear him behind her, groaning, saying something with 'cunt' in it. Feeling triumphant, she remembered her father's repeated advice, "Kick hard and run away." Then she noticed it had suddenly gotten quiet. She stopped and looked behind her. Kyle was gone, and she became aware of the sound of a train coming in the distance, the rails humming, and it got louder with each breath she took. When she turned back toward the street, Kyle was standing in her path again. He smiled and swung an empty wine bottle across her face. She fell back, the blackness already surrounding her.

When she woke, her face stung from the bruise on her cheek. Her head pounded and lifting it made her dizzy. A few mosquitoes were flitting around the blood on her lower lip. The ground was damp and coarse, and she realized her pants and underwear had been pulled off and lay in a pile at her feet. The sky was dark; the moon hid behind a veil of clouds.

Chapter Five

Eddie knocked on Lieutenant Preston's door, a cardboard tomato box under his arm. It was filled with the last of his things: a small desk lamp and a picture someone took at Boston Garden: Eddie and Sam Jones during warm-ups. He was in high school then, fifty pounds ago. The box had paperwork he needed to fill out, two crime novels he never got around to by Chester Himes and Eugene Izzi, a few bottles of aspirin, an unopened split of cheap champagne, a white shirt still in the plastic, and an old leather holster.

Preston opened the door, and stood for a moment holding the doorknob. He was a tall, wide, black man, his usual navy-blue suit, white shirt, and tie. "Come in," he said. "Sit."

Eddie sat in an office chair, Preston behind his desk, a wall of books at his back. He was always reading when he wasn't working. You could catch him at lunchtime holding a book in the diner across the street, or after hours in his office dog-earing a page when you opened the door.

"You look tired, Eddie. Late night?" he asked.

"Couldn't sleep. Too humid."

"Get an air conditioner."

"I can't afford one now."

Preston paused. He didn't say what was on his mind.

"How's the dog track these days?"

"Someone has to feed the puppies, Lieutenant." Eddie shifted in the chair.

Preston let out a short breath. "Do you have everything you need?" he asked.

"Except for a job." Eddie smiled this time, putting an accent on the joke.

Preston looked him deep in his eyes. "This Cronus shit,

Eddie. You need to find a way to let it go."

"We all have ghosts, Lieutenant," he said.

Preston slid him a few pieces of paper, typed, department logo. He put on a pair of reading glasses. "The short version of what you already know. It says you've been on departmental leave for a year, during which time, you were, in part, the subject of an investigation. It also says as a result of a work-related trauma caused by the incident under investigation, it has been determined that the one year leave of absence is to become a permanent disability, effective today."

Eddie stared at the paperwork. He had agreed to the disability because it paid more than retirement, still not enough, but more. He remembered the four trips he had to make to the department shrink for it to become official. The guy was young, about thirty, round glasses and a wall of diplomas. The first visit they talked about what he had seen that night in the marsh, the next visit about his off-duty life, and the last two times they talked about sports for a half an hour. The guy was a Bruins fan, so they didn't have much in common. Neither of them wanted to be there. "You might think about your drinking," he had said, the last day they met.

Preston tapped a finger on the papers. "This isn't about making up," he said. "I wake up every day in the fall still wishing I could play football. Sometimes it's just too fucking bad."

"Please don't give me the line about change being good for me," Eddie snapped.

The room fell silent again. Eddie shuffled the papers.

"This is not easy for me either," Preston said. "But it's necessary. I've seen it happen to too many cops. Use this chance to do yourself some good."

"I didn't fuck up, Lieutenant. That's the sad part. I did my job."

"It's what you *were* doing. A long time before that. You danced on the edge for a while. And…" He leaned into it. "It's how you handled it that night."

The phone rang, and Preston ignored it. "I want you to

hear this," he said. He spoke every word like he'd rehearsed a staged reading. "You could dredge that marsh from now till fucking doomsday and it wouldn't change a thing. It's over. Done. Take your new life and move on."

They shook hands at the door and Eddie walked away with his police life in a box he could mail for three bucks, thinking how much some people know and how much they don't. Preston was smart, Eddie knew that, but Preston didn't know what was in the marsh that night, didn't know what it was like to be haunted by a ghost you knew was real.

After he left the precinct, he drove down the boulevard to the Point of Pines and took a right on Whiten Ave by the G.E. Bridge. He could smell the ocean, see the lazy current moving under the drawbridge. The street was quiet, cars lined on both sides to the curb, a few scattered skinny maple trees on the sidewalks. The houses were all different versions of post-World War II capes cramped together in between single-car driveways.

The school building next to the court looked like it did thirty years ago, an aging monument, the red brick patched in places with rough swaths of cement, the chain-link fence surrounding it clipped with open wounds. He parked next to the basketball court, the asphalt a faded gray on one side, a more recent coat of black on the other, slick scattered puddles from end to end.

Eddie popped the trunk and grabbed a basketball next to the spare tire, a worn leather Wilson he'd had for eight years.

He stood a few feet behind the faded yellow foul line, his fingers gripping the rubber grooves as he eyed the bent rim, the half-moon backboard scratched with graffiti, the chain net. Often he'd done his best thinking on a basketball court, shooting around by himself, sometimes waxing philosophical about the game, what he loved so much about it: the chink of the chain nets, the feel of leather rolling over the fingers.

Maybe he loved it because it might have saved him— the hours he spent here when most kids were finding new ways to break into the neighborhood houses, full-time dopers, and part-time vandals. Some nights he shot baskets until dark while the other kids played *Acey Deucey* and smoked their weed behind the sea wall.

The vision of him thirty years ago shooting free throws while Big Nicky, and a few others huddled on the stone steps with quarters and dimes, was planted in his brain.

He remembered one August day when Nicky got stabbed by a kid from Oak Island and how the kid disappeared after. It happened when you grew up near the beach: people got stabbed, people disappeared, and eventually, people forgot about it.

One more bounce and his memory kept running — a high school tournament game in Boston Garden, his father, his biggest fan, always the loudest voice in the stands, and how he died alone in that condo in Florida. Something inside Eddie felt like it was going to burst. It burned his throat. He swallowed hard, spun the ball in his hands, bent his knees, and his arm shot straight to the rim, his limp wrist posing as the ball fell through the chain net. *Swish.* He thought of his friends and his mother on her death bed, thought of Preston, and their last conversation. Another shot. *Swish.* And another, ten in a row, and he remembered loving the game, the feel of his legs and arms after playing three or four hours, playing in the hot sun, playing on the black ice tar, playing in the dusty gym until the janitor with the whiskey breath kicked them out. Maybe he loved being a cop just as much, even with the drinking always tugging at him.

Then that night a year ago, everything changed. *Cronus.* Their favorite tabloid name. But the image of the Greek God was not the real beast, Eddie knew that. The real one was somewhere under the dirty river, *or was it? Swish.* He knew it would never leave him alone. It would keep calling him, and with the rhythm of one last free throw, he accepted it, the curse he had inherited, and the things it would drive him to do. *Swish.*

Chapter Six
The Beast

When the police came to Kyle Hardy's house around two in the morning, his father, Ray, was passed out in a rocking chair on the porch, his glasses crooked, his hair messed. They searched the house and then John Allen's home in the Pines, and called it in, an eighteen-year-old white male accused of the rape and assault of a fifteen-year-old-girl.

The father gave them a photo, Kyle standing in the backyard with a fishing pole. "This is a few months ago. His friend took it," he said when he handed it over. "He's a time bomb that kid."

People in Oak Island peered out as the police went from one house to the other, three or four cruisers at different times parked in the street, officers in uniform talking to each other, cops on radios talking to other cops out of sight. It was a familiar scene in this neighborhood.

Eddie hadn't thought he would get the call so near the end of his shift. He'd already been drinking for two hours, parked at the circle on the end of the beach, refilling an empty Sprite can with vodka.

He cracked a mint with his teeth and looked at the uniforms standing on the porch of the faded blue house. Then he looked at Gina, the victim, standing in her father's arms on the sidewalk, his eyes full of tears, holding her and rocking back and forth, saying, "My baby, my baby."

Eddie scanned the photo a patrolman was holding (a tall, skinny, eighteen-year-old with long hair). He started down a dark alleyway between two nearby houses, sucking on another mint, and ended up in a backyard. A rusted grill sat on a cement slab patio, a string of burnt-out party lights overhead. At the end of the patio was the dented body of a blue Volkswagen up on blocks.

He circled the backside of the car, pulled a cigarette from the pack in the pocket of his leather jacket, struck a match, then exhaled into the sky. The police blues were still flashing in the neighborhood behind him as he ripped the seal on a nip of vodka and threw it back in two quick swallows. Almost instantly, it burned in his throat and rushed to his head. "Shit," he said, and wobbled.

He flicked the cigarette to the ground, crushed it with his heel, and then saw something move under the V.W. body. When he leaned down to look, he came face to face with a teenage boy staring back at him. The booze, however, had already won this round, and everything started spinning. Eddie stumbled backward, fell to his knees, closed his eyes, and held onto the ground with both hands until it passed.

At one point he thought he felt someone brush by him, but when he opened his eyes and checked the spot under the V.W., the space was empty.

Chapter Seven

Nick Cory shuffled toward the race track exit with the other hollow faces. He stood a head above the crowd, his hair dyed black, dropped a racing program to the floor and tossed the last of his losing tickets in the air.

His blue Ford pickup sat under the lights in the back row of the parking lot. The lot had plenty of spaces closer to the front, but he always parked farther away so he could smoke a joint before he went in without worrying about the cops sneaking up on him. Being high helped him concentrate. It hadn't worked this night; he'd lost eight out of ten and would have to go home and eat spaghetti for a few days.

He'd survive. After all, it was only him now since the bitch ran off.

They'd met at Reardons after a Red Sox's game, slept together for most of the summer; then she moved in when she got kicked out of her apartment for being two months late with the rent. One night, when they were both drunk, he wanted to do something she didn't. "Come on," he said, and she said, "No." And he hit her, closed fist, across the face.

In the morning he told her, "I pay for your cigarettes, the roof over your head. You do what I say."

It was almost three weeks before he hit her a second time.

This night he had stayed until after the last race, wandered around looking on the lobby floor for any change, or loose bills or any uncashed winners dropped by mistake. He was willing to put the leg work in for a free-bee. Last year he made a few thousand on a phone scam, calling elderly ladies and talking them into sending a check for three hundred bucks to protect their social security. He was good at it. *Yes, Mrs. Danforth, especially in this uncertain climate, you need*

26

to protect your investment.

The scam worked with another guy who provided all the phone numbers and cashed the checks. When the guy got nabbed selling drugs out of his apartment (his other part-time gig), the gravy train dried up and Nick had to go back working for the DPW, a job his brother got for him.

One by one, the cars in front of him evaporated, pulling onto the Legion highway. He sparked the half joint left in the ashtray, then started his truck. A strange feeling fell over him, one he was not used to like his luck was about to change. *Maybe if I bring her a six-pack we can kick it up again*, and then he felt it, the pressure against the side of his head, the shattering echo of a gun hammer popping, splitting his eardrum. A rush of bile flew to his mouth, and he slid to the seat, his fingers crawling over the slick blue vinyl. Then nothing.

Chapter Eight
The Beast

A few hours after he assaulted Gina in the Oak Island marsh, Kyle Hardy stood from the cover of the car he was hiding under. He stared as Eddie Devlin stumbled backward on the grass, then he stepped close enough to touch him. "Fucking zombie cop," he said, looking once more at the grown man crouching, eyes closed, and rocking like a baby on the ground.

Kyle kept to the shadows along the Parkway, cut past the oil tanks in Chelsea, and crossed the railroad bridge into East Boston, where he waited for the Blue Line downtown. From there, he made his way to South Station and looked at the board of departures and decided on a bus leaving soon for Portsmouth, New Hampshire. What he'd done to Gina in the marsh was something he couldn't get himself out of, not like when his father paid a cop to beat an assault charge. "You know how much this cost me you piece of shit."

This time was different, but it gave him a reason to run from the place he was sick of anyway. He reached into his pocket and felt the fold of new bills he'd taken from his father's dresser.

"Who's the piece of shit now?" he whispered.

In Portsmouth, he spent a night sleeping behind the tankers off the highway. In the morning, he ditched the cowboy boots for a pair of sneakers in the gym bag he slept on, smoked his last joint, and hitchhiked his way to the White Mountains, about two hours north. A German couple in a blue Volvo picked him up on their way to Canada and drove him to the doorstep of the Joe Dodge Lodge, near the base of Wild Cat Mountain. His parents had brought him here a few times, summers when he was younger, and he remembered the waterfall a half-mile up toward Tuckerman Ravine, where he'd thrown rocks into the spray.

He spent a few days eating in the cafeteria, walking the trails on either side of the road, and sleeping at night in the open cars of people off to the overnight huts.

One afternoon, as the sun was heading down over Wild Cat, he hiked across to Square Ledge (about eight-hundred feet above the road) and sat alone until the stars came out. He thought a few times about what he'd done to Gina, how it felt to have her that way, to be able to do anything he wanted. Remembering the control of it almost got him off.

The next day he met a guy in the cafeteria who lived an hour north in Whitefield. He was older, said he ran a carpet laying company, and was always looking for extra help. The guy agreed to let him rent a room in his basement until he could afford his own place.

They smoked a joint together on the ride there. Kyle took a new name, Kenny Talbot, said he was from Florida, "Ocala," he said. The guy talked about hiking, how it cleared his head from the day to day junk, about his wife, who divorced him three years before, and about his business and how it wasn't that hard once you learned how to measure and use the hooked carpet knife.

Chapter Nine

Eddie woke around noontime, stretched out on the couch; the TV weatherman were going on about more rain. He scanned the apartment to get his bearings. The place was pretty empty. In addition to the couch he was on, Eddie owned a bed, a kitchen table, a floor lamp, and a plywood dresser his landlord (who lived most of the year in Florida) let him have.

He stood, separated the blinds, and looked out the window. Last night was a blur; he remembered sitting in the driveway staring at the yellow-stucco two-family where he lived, listening to the traffic crossing the G.E. Bridge a few blocks away, then watching a western with Dean Martin and Walter Brennon before he nodded off to sleep.

After a cup of instant coffee and a day-old blueberry muffin, he pulled on a pair of sneakers. When he bent to tie the laces, he felt a familiar pain in the back of his head. "Shit," he whispered.

The sky was still full of dark clouds as he drove down Broadway, but there was a break in the rain. He killed the wipers. The driver side only worked occasionally anyway.

He passed the housing projects on Adams, the rows of brick fronts, patio stoops crowded with trash bags and broken appliances, bicycles and plastic toys strewn about the small brown spots of lawn. After crossing the traffic circle onto the Marsh Road, he felt the slight numb hush that made it seem that things were okay. Then he saw the chain-link fence and the stacked car bodies and the piles of scrap a hundred yards in front of him. A dark spot in his gut rose to his throat. He pulled past the worn wooden junkyard gates that were always open as if the junk business was a twenty-four-hour convenience store.

Roman was standing on the steps by the door of his trailer under a green, corrugated porch roof, wearing a sleeveless white tee shirt. His hair and beard resembled a wild black mane, and his belly drooped over a carnival belt buckle. Eddie hated him, his biker tattoos, the way he talked, his penchant for teenage girls too stupid or too messed up to run the other way when they saw him coming. One time, Eddie told Preston that Roman was 'the go-to guy on the scum bag all-star team.'

He nosed the car tight enough to a parked Harley to get Roman's attention. *One more time*, he thought, reaching for the thin, worn leather jacket in the back seat. He opened the door and got out.

"Well, well," Roman said, smiling. "Long time no see. What it's been, five days?"

"Fuck you," Eddie snapped, putting the jacket on. Closer to him now, he could smell cheap deodorant and tobacco.

"Don't you get tired of beating a dead horse?" Roman asked.

"Maybe I should try beating a dead biker."

Roman laughed, his stomach shaking. "Careful, Detective. I heard you might not have a badge to hide behind."

Eddie walked off into the yard, past the dead bodies of burnt cars, the piles of rubber tires. Something moved under a hub cap, probably a rat or a cat, or maybe a junkyard ghost.

They both knew where Eddie was going, to the back corner of the lot where the white Buick still escaped getting crushed, only because Eddie told Roman he'd kill him if he did it.

"That would be murder?" Roman had said.

"Any reason," Eddie had fired back, "would be justice."

He couldn't prove Roman had ever killed anyone, but he knew he was a scum bag who threw his weight around when he had ten of his friends with him. Eddie was sure he'd had his hands into more than one young girl dropping charges against one of his slug friends, or some guy who owed him drug money getting his teeth bashed in. Like most thugs, Eddie figured he was a coward and a bully. Killing him

31

wasn't something he thought he'd ever really do, but wanting to kill him seemed to be the right thing to think about.

About twenty cars in the back of the yard were waiting to be crushed for whatever reason Roman invented or got paid to invent. At the end of the line, a few spaces removed from the rest was a white Buick Skylark. The department had it towed there after they combed through it and ripped out the guts. Eddie circled the car, studying it as if it were a museum piece or a gemstone that could give him answers. Maybe it would show him a vision of a corpse in that stinking marsh, buried like a nut in a Christmas fruit cake.

His muscles tightened, and he knew what the nuns had told him about purgatory was true. He was living it. When he closed his eyes, he imagined the parts of the story he couldn't know— Michelle Letti drinking with her friend, a going-away party at the China Jade just over the G.E. Bridge, *I'm going to miss you bitch,* on her way to Florida, a new life, a second chance maybe. They probably hugged in the parking lot, then Michelle drove the marsh road, singing along to a song, perhaps The Supremes. A sudden bang and she pulled the car to the shoulder, the flat tire, the rain spitting into the dark. Did she walk towards the lights a few miles away, until a sound made her turn to the marsh, something blurry in the shadows, then the first sharp spike, then another…She must have fallen to her knees, the warm blood oozing through her fingers. Before she knew what was happening, was she being pulled by the neck of her sweatshirt, the cold, wet grass underneath her frozen arms, her shoes slipping off one by one, her heels digging into the mud? She might have looked into the sky at a plane flying overhead on the way to East Boston, and gasped for a breath that didn't come, and heard someone speaking to her, a low moan, almost a chant as her ears filled with a loud hum. And just before the blackness, did she think of lying on a beach in the hot sun?

He stayed for the usual twenty minutes.

By the time he walked back to his own car, Roman was with two other biker buddies, both wearing sleeveless leather vests over skinny chests. The three of them sat smoking on the steps to the trailer.

Roman spoke for them. "Find what you're looking for, Detective?"

Eddie stopped at the car door.

"Or what should I call you these days?" Roman laughed and one of his friends blew a smoke ring. Eddie had his hand on the door handle. *Just get in the car. Another time.* Roman whispered something to his boys, and they smiled back as if they were posing for a photo. One of them laughed out loud.

Eddie got in and started the car. He looked at the three Harleys parked in front of the trailer, then hit the gas and clipped the first bike, sending it crashing into the other two. Roman and his crew scampered up to the doorway as Eddie backed up twenty feet or so and punched the gas again, pushing the tangled pile of bikes with his bumper. The chrome scraped against the ground, and a cloud of dust rose over the pile. Roman and his friends glared back, and Eddie leaned out the window. "Call me daddy, pig boy."

He put the car in reverse and fish-tailed into a one-eighty and headed out the gates watching in the rearview mirror as the three men pulled the bikes apart yelling something he couldn't quite hear, but something he was sure he would have enjoyed if he was in a better mood.

Chapter Ten

Preston got the call that afternoon, sent two more cars to rope things off, and moved the news people as far back as possible. He knew he'd have to spin this thing quickly before it got too tabloid. He could only imagine the circus that was coming to town. *Another marsh murder. Cronus? Whatever happened to Eddie Devlin?*

Nick Cory's blue Ford pickup was nowhere in sight, though there were tire tracks in the mud. His body was found by a kid from Oak Island walking back with a fishing pole from Dizzy Bridge. Cory had been rolled into the first cut of weeds, one leg in the wet brown water, the other on the damp ground, almost like he was crawling out of the swamp when he died. One side of his head was ripped open, a small bullet sized puncture on the other.

Preston stood in the middle of the uniforms moving around him as if he were a statue in a blue department slicker. He heard one patrolman say as they zipped up the body bag, "he must have blown his stack over something." Preston knew this sense of humor. He'd been guilty of it himself, a way of dealing with the things that were too real, too often.

Stepping carefully on the mushy turf under his feet, he waved his big hand in the air and yelled, "This fucking place is trampled."

A hawk circled overhead, wings gliding softly on the currents. Preston stared at it, thinking of Eddie Devlin and how this might affect him, almost a year to the date. He liked Eddie, even if he figured a lot of his trouble was his own doing. Preston was a self-disciplined guy; he only had so much sympathy. Sure, he threw a few back, but never more than a few and never more than once or twice a week. He watched what he ate, exercised some, enough to satisfy a stress test. It was up to each man he believed, to make a difference in his life. *We all have our demons.* As much as he wanted to help Eddie, he was tired of a guy who couldn't get out of his own way.

"Clean this up and keep the news back," he said, watching the hawk dive to the marsh and scoop a field mouse in full run. He kept watching as the hawk's wings vaporized into the clouds, beyond the marsh and the cars moving in a slow line over the hill on Route One, beyond the smoke from the junkyard that was blowing downwind.

Chapter Eleven

The beach spread out at the bottom of the Shirley Ave hill, a wispy surf banging against the seawall. Eddie rolled past the Vietnamese storefronts, *cigarettes, lottery, newspapers,* pulled the car to the curb in front of a brick triple-decker, number thirteen. He took the bag of groceries he'd picked up at Giovanni's and hustled into the foyer and pressed the intercom.

"You decent?" he asked.

"Depends who's asking," a woman's voice said.

"I've got food."

"Then no, I'm not."

When he walked into the first-floor hallway, he could hear the music from the slightly open door about halfway down the scuffed green carpet, *Sonny Rollins, the early years,* her favorite. The smooth sax pulled him like a train ticket home past the faded brown wallpaper, the other nondescript door fronts. He pushed the door open into the tiny living room, a few cheap oil paintings of the beach on the far wall, a matching green couch and chair, and a Zenith television set that looked like it needed a funky circle antenna to get any channel with a hockey game. Gwendolyn was sitting in her wheelchair next to the counter, cutting fruit, her black hair pulled tight on her head, showing off the olive glow of her cheeks. She was wearing a bright flowered shirt and a white skirt.

"Turn the light down," Eddie said, looking at the shirt.

"I like it," she told him. "It's cheery." She held the corner of it and looked down. "I got it at a yard sale."

"No doubt," Eddie said, put the bag on the counter and kissed her on the forehead. "Sorry, I'm late, but I brought pasta."

Gwen rolled her eyes. "If you don't stop with the starch I'll be stuck in this chair."

"*Mangia, mangia*," Eddie said.

He sat on the two-seat sofa, looked at the framed photo next to the television— Gwen's father in a yellow suit coat, smooth, dark skin, standing on a beach in the Dominican Republic.

"Well," she said, emptying the bag, "is it settling in?" She watched closely for an answer. "I haven't heard from you all week."

They looked at each other.

"It's not like I didn't know what was coming," he said. "Just a formality."

She stopped what she was doing. "I didn't ask that."

Gwendolyn was no-nonsense, and the bravest person Eddie knew. There wasn't much he hadn't run by her over the years, the things that haunted him: a baby beaten to death for crying, a jealous lover with a hammer, the remnants of a gunfight.

She ran a clinic for rape survivors. When she was twenty-five, she was raped by two men in her Revere Street apartment. She fought and tried to escape, but fell two flights of stairs and snapped her spine. They never found the men.

Eddie had been on the detail a few times when she spoke in one of the city's church basements. "This chair reminds me every day of the violation," she'd tell a room full of victims. "We've all been violated. Together we can make progress, get our lives back. If I can do it, you can do it."

One night he asked her to a double feature in Cambridge. They had coffee and pie in an all-night diner after. The conversation came easy, so they did it again a couple of weeks later. That was a few years ago now. They might have even been something like boyfriend and girlfriend if Eddie hadn't been too much to handle. He knew it, and *she* knew it, but he was loyal to her, and in return she kept him grounded on his worst days.

"I've been to the marsh again," he said. He was there

almost every day, but he didn't tell her that.

Gwen wheeled into the room.

"I parked and looked for about an hour." He sucked a deep breath. "The job, the end of it, is bringing it all back."

"What do you expect to find there?" she asked.

"I don't know. It's like I'm waiting to remember something. That's how it feels anyway."

"Come," she told him.

Eddie swung his feet across the couch and lay back. Gwen tucked the wheelchair into the sidearm and placed her hands under his head. He could hear her breathing when he closed his eyes, the warmth of her hands on his neck.

They sat that way for several minutes, eyes closed, pasta boiling, Sonny Rollins on the record player.

"Say it," she said.

"The demon is dead," he whispered.

"Again."

"The demon is dead," Eddie repeated, softer this time, then he felt himself falling into oblivion and leaving it all behind, the rain, the nightmare, the checkered shirt beast running around the marsh like a champion.

Chapter Twelve
The Beast

Kyle disappeared into his life in the mountains.

He lived in the basement below his boss, was always on time, and got better with the measuring and cutting after a few weeks. The first job he did on his own, he cut a living room rug seven-eighths the size of the room, but his boss sold the woman on the strip of natural wood left uncovered, called it an 'entrance piece', said a lot of people were doing it for effect. She bought it. They laughed about it in the truck on the way home. "You got to give em what they want, or you got to tell them what they need," his boss said, sipping a can of cold beer.

After work, Kyle kept mostly to himself, managed to save money to buy weed from a guy his boss knew, bought new work boots and jeans, and a jacket for the winter. He spent nights smoking in the basement, listening to music, thinking about biding his time until something showed itself, like that night in the marsh, something helpless.

He knew a few guys that worked on the ski mountain, Bretton Woods, but they were here one day and gone the next. It didn't matter to him; he was used to coexisting without really having friends. Even the kids back in Oak Island kept him at arm's length. The few who hung with him were always watching their back, and no one wanted their sister to go near him.

John Allen from the Pines was maybe his only friend from Revere, or Kyle's cousin Kenny. Kenny came from Florida to visit for a few weeks every summer. They'd go to the beach and spend all day at the arcades or eat pizza on the sea wall. They talked about girls and baseball. Kenny told him his plans for his life when he got older, how he was going to own

39

a construction company in Ocala like his old man so that he could have nice cars and a big house and tons of girlfriends. Kyle liked the way he talked about it, sure of himself, and certain that the big payday was out there waiting for him.

But that all changed after Kyle's mother decided to split up with his father and that side of the family stopped visiting.

The night she left, Kyle heard a bottle smash, his mother scream, then a car pulling up outside. She came into the bedroom and kissed him on the forehead, "I'll call you when I'm settled. You can come then." But that phone call never came.

A few years later Kyle heard that Kenny had joined the Marines and was killed driving a jeep into a ditch. One night drinking with his father, he said out of the blue, "and that Kenny thought he was so fucking great, ha."

Chapter Thirteen

Eddie removed the damp black leather jacket and slung it over his shoulder as he walked up the ramp of the dog track. His stomach was full from three plates of pasta at Gwen's and he moved slowly into the lobby. It dawned on him how gray this place was: gray cement floors, gray painted counters where people scribbled notes in the margins of their racebooks, which dogs ran wide, which ones liked the mud. Even the people walking back and forth muttering to themselves looked gray, most of them smoking, the tobacco clouds above their heads sucking them toward some fatal collision with luck.

He knew these people: eyed the spot on the back of the infield where the off-duty Revere cops hung out (a section he avoided). The Vietnamese guys from the Ave huddled by a bank of TVs, the G.E. workers stood next to the clubhouse doors, and the vets from the VFW in Chelsea hung by the coffee counter.

No surprises here. If you won, you'd hand it back; that was the deal. He had plenty of reasons to stay away: too bright, too much smoke, too many familiar faces. But with all that knowledge in his cap, he still managed to come to the window, two twenties in hand, and a list of daily double combinations. It was bad religion and he couldn't imagine going too long without it.

At the back of the infield, he leaned against the glass doors, watched the greyhounds explode from the gate. The ground at his feet was littered with dead tickets like the day after a V- Day parade. In front of him, the matinee dogs chased the metal rabbit to the roar of the crowd. Numbers shuffled over the tote board in the distance, like some hypnotist trick, the hum of the people yelling, "Come on you mother." A late hush, a few joyous screams of, "Yes, yes." Then he wandered to the window and said to the gray-haired teller, "Next race, five on the nose."

In the back of the bar, under low lights, he saw Dana and a couple of regulars. Dana had the pink sheet, the one with the latest insider tips. He was waving it like a fan. "This is all it's good for," he said. "This and wiping your ass."

The two guys laughed, local runners from Revere Street, mostly made their buck off the street number. Like many of Dana's clients they had no real money but wore a lot of jewelry and always had a fresh haircut.

Both guys were Dana disciples, leaned on his every word like he was some Zen master of the racetrack. Eddie always thought it funny that people thought Dana knew so much about the horses and the dogs. He was like any good gambler, told you about his winnings but didn't say much about the ones that got away. The record was inflated.

"The King and his court," Eddie said, interrupting the sacred circle.

"How goes it?" Dana asked.

One of the guys leaned in, "Hey, you ain't a cop no more I heard."

Dana looked at Eddie, then back at the guy. "Go find a hole to crawl in."

"What?" the guy said, his buddy walking him away.

"Sprinkle us," Dana said to the bartender.

"How you doing?" Dana asked.

"It's official."

"You want to go eat somewhere or something?"

"You don't want to see a grown man cry, do you?" Eddie looked at him, cracked a smile, then turned away and scanned the large room, tables and chairs, and race sheets, people scurrying back and forth before the window closed. For a second, they looked like ants.

Eddie walked to the glass as the race call went off. *There goes Swifty.*

The five dog, a brown coat, black spots around the thigh, a

green number five jacket, flew out of the gate, his snout pulsing through the brown leather, his clipped ears flat to his head. He flew through the first turn with a four-length lead and stayed that way until the halfway mark when he opened it to seven.

Eddie had him tight in his sight, the dog looking smooth, then he saw it, the slight stumble followed instantly by the flip that took out four other dogs, their lean bodies scattered in three directions. The two bumped wide to the rail, the five and the three hobbled across the finish line like revolutionary soldiers he'd seen in a painting once, bandaged and broken.

He ripped the tickets and put them on the bar. The boys and Dana were back at the book.

It reminded him of a horse joke Dana told one night. A guy watches the horses trotting to the starting gate. One by one they strut by and the seven-horse winks. They circle one more time and the seven-horse winks again. The guy runs to the window and bets the house. The seven finishes dead last. As the horses walk back to the paddock, the seven looks at the guy and shrugs his shoulders.

After one more race, he met Dana coming back from the window.

"I'm heading out," Eddie said.

"Early exit. You must have won big."

"Just not feeling it."

"On the bad days," Dana said, "I think of my grandfather. He used to say, 'at least you got a shot that tomorrow will be better.'"

"Is that hope?" Eddie asked.

"Who knows?" Dana said. "He got hit by a bus leaving a Bingo night."

"Not such a bad way to go," Eddie said.

"Better than a shark attack, I guess."

"Was he happy… before that?" Eddie asked.

Dana thought about it. "No. He was pretty miserable."

"Maybe he never found what he was looking for."

"I know he wasn't looking when he crossed the street," he said. "Be at the bar later?"

"We'll see," Eddie said and walked away, the people crisscrossing the gray floor around him on their way to the widows.

Driving home, Eddie thought about how he had nights like this too often, returning to an empty pad, sitting on the couch drinking alone, going over it all again in his head, the weeks after Michelle Letti and the Cronus murder. "I was a prisoner in my own station house," he'd told Dana, "answering questions from detectives I'd worked with for fifteen years, then the Lieutenant, then the outside brass."

"Fuck them," Dana had said, but Eddie remembered the two guys with crew cuts and black suits, the taller one asking all the questions.

"Were you drunk?"

"I'd had a few."

"Were you drunk?"

"No."

"Again, why did you move the body?"

The truth was he couldn't remember why. He was sure if he hadn't been drinking, it would have been standard procedure. But something about her lying there, this young girl, someone's friend, someone's daughter, a few feet from the man who had just... He couldn't do it.

Ron Fisher had shown up that night, pulled him aside, the rain bouncing off his new whiffle cut. "Eddie, is there something I should know? Now's the time to tell me."

"What the fuck are you saying?"

"There's no body. Just the girl."

Eddie had run back into the swamp, past a uniform who tried to stop him from stomping through the crime scene. He made it all the way to the water, stepped knee-deep in the rising scum, looking left and right, scooping his arms like he was fishing for something swimming around his ankles.

By the time they wrestled him back to the street, Preston was there and guided him by the arm into a cruiser and shut the door. The scene outside was blurred, people milling about, some pointing back at Eddie's face against the glass,

Preston's voice rising above the fray.

Fisher took him home and offered to come in but Eddie said no.

"Nine o'clock with the boss man," he reminded him, and Eddie walked the driveway to his apartment, slow, heavy steps, like a man walking uphill after a long time on the road.

Inside he pulled the cork from a bottle of wine, then fished in his cabinet for whatever was left. He spent the night pacing and smoking, then sitting on the couch by the television but never turned it on. *Fuck the news*, he figured. He would have called Gwen if he knew what to say. "Fuck that too," he said as if he was convincing someone standing over his shoulder. Eventually he got drunk enough to fall asleep on the couch.

The phone rang at eight in the morning.

"You ready for this?" Fisher asked.

"Do I have a choice?" Eddie answered.

"Your car is out front."

"Is it dusted?"

"They're not saying that. You know how it is. This job sucks most of the time," Fisher said.

Eddie was silent.

"But we're the last line of defense, right," Fisher said. "We speak for the dead."

"Real heroes," Eddie said.

Fisher might have been one of the good ones. Who knew? But they had a history before they both ended up police. Most of it revolved around basketball in the city as kids (Eddie kicking his ass too many times) and one late-night fight outside a barroom on the beach when they were just out of high school, the two of them rolling around the gravel parking lot for ten minutes. Years later, his first day on the force, Ron came up to him and said, "Well, well, who would have ever thunk it? The two of us wearing the same badge."

Eddie knew there had been two bodies in the marsh that night, the murderer and the victim. He also knew what the papers were saying, the questions already circulating with each new edition, the ones the department refused to answer, reciting 'the ongoing investigation' line. A week after it happened, Eddie was walking past two drunks sitting under one of the pavilions on the beach. One of them talked about a night club comic at the strip joint on Ocean Ave who told a joke about a cop who shot a guy and lost the body. "Come on," the joke went, "it's not like it's a fucking wristwatch."

Michelle Letti's body not even cold, and Eddie had already become a punch line.

Chapter Fourteen

Preston made his way through the ranks of the Revere Police Department mostly out of spite. He took every exam, went to every seminar, worked the very streets where he might go two hours without seeing another black man. It was a different scene from Lynn, the next city north of Revere, where he grew up.

He played high school football for The Lynn English Bulldogs, a two-way tackle for four years. They double and triple-teamed him to keep him out of the backfield. In his last game his senior year, a game he already had twelve tackles in, a letter signed for a full scholarship to Michigan, two kids from the Saugus High football team cut him at the knee, one in front, one behind, and his leg snapped loud enough that people heard it fifteen rows into the stands.

After high school, he lived at the YMCA in Beachmont near the subway at the end of the strip. He paid for the room (plus a little) by checking people in and out, keeping watch over the weight room when he wasn't in Boston taking classes at Suffolk University. He threw a guy out one day for starting a fight, and later that night the guy came back with two of his friends. They beat him with bats until he was unconscious. Before Preston blacked out however, he got one of the bats away and was sure he did some damage. When the police came, they said there was nothing they could do. "Besides," one of them said, "you're a big boy. You'll be okay."

Preston waited for the next police exam and took it. He was denied the first time, and the next two times after that. Years later, he wondered what he was trying to prove; did he want to make things right for himself, or the next guy or was he just pissed off?

Finally, five years later, when he graduated from college, he was put on the force for good.

At the corner of Revere Street and the boulevard, Preston stopped walking, the memories clinging to him like the humidity. He looked up at the purple neon sign above the door, *Sam's Lounge,* a once part-time biker bar, now a local live band joint that served pizza.

The lounge inside was one large dark room with white round tables and few vinyl-padded booths along the wood-paneling. A foot-high stage was set up against the windows on the beachside, a sign hanging behind the drum set for a band called *Sass.*

Preston nodded to the thick, bald guy behind the bar. "Busy?"

"Making a buck."

"Wish I could say the same," he said, spotting Ron Fisher reading a newspaper in a booth against the far wall. "One beer, one Coke," he ordered..

He carried the bottles to the booth. Fisher looked up from the paper and smiled. He was tanned with close-cropped silver hair. "Lieutenant."

Preston sat and slid the Coke over. "How you doing?"

"Taking nourishment," Fisher said, putting his hand around the bottle, his taut muscles evident through the tight white sweater. "This on you or the department?"

"I'll put in for it, don't worry," Preston said.

"Thank God for the taxpayer." Fisher smiled again and picked up the paper and turned it to a photo of the marsh, the police standing over the corpse still clinging to the swamp grass. The headline read, *Cronus Returns?* "Interesting reading," he said.

Preston stared at him, straight-faced. "We've got a problem."

"We?" Fisher asked, his face suddenly turning sour. "That guy was a dirtball. You should be happy?"

"Dirtball or no." Preston sipped his beer. "I'm not crying

over this punk either..." A bottle dropped behind the bar followed by someone yelling, *shit*. "I've got a feeling this is going to fall back in my lap."

"So what do you want from me?" Fisher asked.

"I want to nip it the bud. Or at least find out quietly that's it's not what I think it is."

"Why quietly?"

"He's a cop. Just like you."

Fisher grabbed Preston's beer and peeled the label from the bottle. "I take it you want to know either way," he said. He put the label back upside down on the bottle.

"Before anyone else."

"What if you find out he's bonkers?"

"Is that a prediction?" Preston asked. "From a man who doesn't like him."

"Two years ago, a young woman comes into the station with a black eye," Fisher said. "She files a complaint against her boyfriend, Nick Cory. Eddie takes the compliant, gives her a coffee, and just before she leaves, he asks where Cory hangs out."

"So?" Preston said.

"She dropped the complaint, but I heard later the boyfriend got a talking to, up close and personal."

"Sounds like police work to me."

Fisher finished his Coke and folded the newspaper. "I also hear he spends a lot of time in the marsh since..." he leaned across the table and whispered, "the incident."

Preston looked back.

"...and he visits the car in the junkyard. Told Roman he'd kill him if he demo'd it."

"Those things don't make him a murderer."

"They could make him fucking nuts. My bet is he's looking for a ghost, so what does he do? He conjures one up." Fisher stood, lightly slapped Preston on the shoulder. "Or not. I've been wrong before. Get some sleep. I'll look into it."

That's what Ron Fisher did. He looked into things the force didn't want any tag on. Occasionally he crawled out of the woodwork if Preston stamped on the floor hard enough. It could be guys cutting detail and getting paid, the occasional cop selling drugs, or just some pet project that Preston wanted to handle in house. They weren't friends, but they understood each other. Fisher had 'officially' retired a few years ago after a shooting put him behind a desk. He was just invisible enough to get whatever Preston needed. He wore the different hats well, sometimes holding a cop's hand long enough to get the goods to fry him. It wasn't free, but Preston had enough 'funny money' for rainy days like this.

He watched Fisher move through the empty barroom, limping slightly with each step, the permanent traces of some wise guy's bullet. He knew he'd sent Fisher on a mission to spy on someone else he'd known for a long time. It made him ask, "why would anyone do this for a living?" Then he thought back to his first day on the job when he overheard two detectives talking about a stand on the beach back in the old days. One of them said, "ya, you could throw baseballs at a black man for five cents a try. Hit the coon in the head, win a prize." He had said it loud enough for Preston to hear.

Something to prove? There was always that.

Chapter Fifteen

Pudge Bankia stared at the television set in the corner of the *Driftwood* bar, thinking of a kid who owed him money for a pile of black beauties. A tall bartender with a beard poured some scotch into a glass in front of him.

"If you see your brother," Bankia said to the bartender, "tell him I was here."

"For what?" the bartender asked.

"He'll know."

The intro to *Charlie's Angels* flashed across the TV screen. "I'd do them all at once," Bankia said, then laughed, but the bartender had already moved away. He sipped the last of his scotch and water, left a meager tip, and walked out to the boulevard. A few cars sped past as he waited to cross the street where his purple El Dorado was parked.

Bankia was no stranger to this beach. He'd had odd jobs as a kid, hung out at the arcade, and used his big body to scare kids into giving him their quarters. When he got older, he got his electrician's license and worked when he had to. He sold drugs most of the time, switched from beating up kids on the beach to beating his girlfriends. One night he punched his mother in the face for calling him a pig.

Everybody knew what a scumbag he was, but the cops always failed to find anything that could stick. He spent most of his time looking for young girls hooked on dope. Lately he'd been dancing with jail time again. A young girl died in an apartment on Shirley Ave from an overdose of cocaine. They had Bankia all over the apartment, his prints, his dope, his semen. But again, he walked.

He sat behind the wheel, adjusted the rearview mirror, and a voice from the back said, "Drive."

When he turned to make a move, a gun barrel pinched his cheek.

"Turn the fuck around…and drive," the voice said.

Bankia started the car and pulled out. "Where to?" he asked.

"Up the boulevard and turn onto the Marsh Road," the voice told him. "Nice and slow."

Chapter Sixteen
The Beast

Kyle had become invisible, melted into the mountains like another transplanted flat-lander. He did his business and then disappeared into the shadows of the conifers, the trails, the resort barrooms. For months, he installed carpet in the day and went back to being a stranger to nearly everybody at night. Then the day came when he started hanging with some of the locals at a bowling alley where he played pool now and then. This one night, a kid named Murry, who made his living selling weed and teaching skiing in the winter, invited him to his apartment to smoke pot and watch Miami Vice and Monty Python. A couple of girls from Conway, the next town over, came along too. Everyone got pretty toasted, and Kyle watched the girl with the long blonde hair sitting across from him. She was wearing a white tee-shirt. "White and tight," he whispered to himself.

Murry leaned over and said something to the girl, and she winked at Kyle. A few seconds later, when she walked outside, he followed her, lightly grabbed a fistful of her hair.

"Hey, what do you think you're doing?" she asked him.

"I don't know," Kyle said. "What do you want me to do?"

She smiled a little and turned toward him. "What do you got?" she said, looking down. "Let's see."

"Self-serve," Kyle told her.

"Oh no. You want it, you take it out." She put her hands on her hips, watched as Kyle awkwardly unzipped his fly.

"Pull your pants down," she told him.

"The mosquitoes," he said.

She stepped right up to him. "You want it or what?"

He pushed his jeans down to his knees, then his shorts,

shivered a little in the late-night mountain air. The girl took one step closer, put her hands on his waist and said, "Loverboy," then pushed him backward.

Murry, who had snuck up behind him, was kneeling on all fours and Kyle's legs flew out from under him and he landed hard on the ground, the twigs and the damp dirt sticking to him. Murry and the girls stood laughing as he struggled to his feet and pulled up his pants, his long hair hanging in his face.

He spit at them. "Assholes," he yelled.

"We were just playing," Murry said. "You should have seen your face."

They all laughed again.

Kyle charged them, already swinging his fist. The girls ducked away, but Murry stepped into him, knocked him to the ground, and knelt on his shoulders.

"Cool it, man," he said. "It was a joke."

"Fuck you," Kyle said and swung a glancing blow to Murry's chin. Murry punched him square in the nose, then backed off. Kyle moaned, and the blood flowed in two slight streams to his lips. He rolled over and spat into the dirt.

When he stood up, the blood ran down his chin.

The others watched him in silence.

"Hey man," Murry said. "Sorry about that but you were looking crazy."

Kyle stared at him, not bothering to wipe his face, a few slight red pools forming at his feet.

"Come on in," the girl said. "We'll fix you up."

Kyle smiled, his yellow teeth, outlined in red. "No worry," he said like he was talking to nobody. "We were just playing, right?" He walked away.

They called to him, but he stopped listening after a few steps, moving further into the darkness and away from their voices. Soon all he heard were his feet crunching on the leaves and the bugs buzzing in his ears all the way to the highway.

Chapter Seventeen

Eddie woke from a nightmare: he had been submerged under the thick, wet earth of the marsh. His father, dressed as a judge, was tamping the dirt above his head with a shovel.

He couldn't get back to sleep after, so he paced around the apartment thinking about being officially removed from the job and how the news of a recent marsh murder in the papers might make him a household name again.

Staring out the living room window into the darkness, he thought about all the shit he'd seen on this beach over the years: the biker bars and the discos, the wise guys, the hippies, the drugs, the beach always on the brink of boil. This much was true: people died on the beach every few months for reasons guys in jail couldn't even remember.

He picked up a half-full bottle of vodka from the kitchen counter and poured it into the sink. Then he reached above to the cabinet, grabbed another bottle, and poured that out too. He moved around the kitchen, opening drawers, putting nip bottles on the counter, pulling cans of beer from the fridge. By the time he finished, he had a paper bag full of bottles and cans that he carried to the back hallway.

This wasn't the first time he'd performed this ritual. Booze, he knew, had caused most of the turmoil in his life. He wasn't stupid, but he never went into a moment like this thinking long term. Like the other times he'd gone on the wagon, he ended up at the kitchen table afterward, rethinking his decision.

Eventually he settled into the couch in the living room and watched an old gangster movie, *White Heat*, with James Cagney. Like Cagney, he could sometimes picture himself standing on top of a compressed gas silo, firing his weapon at his feet and sending himself into oblivion.

In the morning, he drove past the junkyard on his way to the market. Roman was stepping out of his tow truck by the open gate. Eddie honked as he drove past. Roman lowered his dark sunglasses, recognized the car, and flashed him the finger. Eddie knew he'd come calling someday for smashing up his bike now that there was no badge between them. In a way, he welcomed it.

He was smiling, still thinking about those bikes sprawling in the dust, when he passed the circle on the beach, just outside of Beachmont. There was a white stucco building on the corner set back against the train tracks. The paint was peeling, and the asphalt parking lot had grass growing through the cracks, and a tall, broken neon sign read: *The Surf Club. All Day Dancers.*

Eddie's second night on the force, they called him from there just before his duty was up, about three in the morning. The place was closed. A few cars were parked in the lot next to an RPD cruiser.

Preston met him at the front door. "I need you to look at something," he said and led Eddie inside, past the red-clothed tables and the empty stage. A big guy with a long ponytail was stocking bottles at the bar; otherwise, the place was empty.

"What happened?" Eddie asked.

"You tell me," Preston said and kept walking a few paces ahead of him.

They turned a corner and down a dark hallway, then stopped by a red door. Preston pushed it open. "We have a delicate situation here," he said and led him into a dressing room with a wall of mirrors and a red velvet couch. A woman was sitting with her head in her hands, long black hair, and a thin blue robe. She appeared to be sobbing. When she stood up, she said, "Yes, a situation." Her robe fell to the floor exposing her breasts and a tiny purple G-string.

The door shut behind him and when Eddie turned toward it, Preston stood there laughing with another cop. It was Ron Fisher.

The girl moved closer. "Well," she said, biting her lip. "Can you help me with my situation?" She pressed against his uniform as he heard the others leaving.

"Be nice to him, Janice," Fisher said. "He's only a baby."

Chapter Eighteen

Preston hung up the phone, leaned back in his chair and let out a long tired breath. The papers had called already; *Cronus* was leading every evening edition. He knew this road too well and it never ended with the department looking good. The local news trucks were already on the scene. Once the national guys got hold of it, Revere would be in dinner conversations from New York to Maine. *Fuck, people will be writing books about it*, Preston thought.

The landscape ahead was fraught with the timely tics that made his life miserable. Bad enough the city had two people getting killed a few days apart, but both bodies ending up in the same place in the marsh made this a newsman's dream and Eddie Devlin a tabloid player. Whoever did this knew what they were doing, and when Preston found out, he was going to make it personal.

The mayor had just visited a half an hour earlier. "You got one on your hands now, Lieutenant."

"No kidding," Preston had said.

"The city already has a ring around its collar?"

"And no amount of cliché is going to solve it, Mayor."

"You know what I mean. Stop this shit before it gets out of control. I don't want them banging down the front door of city hall."

"Not any more than I want you banging on mine," Preston said.

"You'll be hearing from me, Al," the mayor said.

"No doubt."

Preston had backed the Irish kid, Fitzgerald, in the election a year ago. The mayor never let him forget it.

Earlier, Preston had stood over Pudge Bankia's body, face

down in the marsh mud, a bullet hole clean through his brain back to front, about fifty yards from the last body left there. The Medical Examiner figured he was twenty-four hours dead when they found him. His purple El Dorado was parked a hundred yards away on the gravel shoulder. Preston had taken it all in, the caution tape waving in the wind, the usual people moving back and forth, each trying to be more important than the next. The rain had stopped, but it felt like it could pour any minute. He had looked at the gray sky and back at the body, another neat headshot, execution style. It was like a dream he could not shake, and he kept thinking about Eddie and their last conversation, the way he looked leaving the office; *we all have ghosts, Lieutenant.*

Chapter Nineteen
The Beast

Four days after Kyle partied at Murry's apartment, he bought some new black army boots, a pair of jeans, and a new red flannel shirt. He threw the new clothes into a small gym bag, left the level and the measuring tape on the floor by his bed, but kept the carpet knife in the leather case on his belt.

He never told the old man he was leaving.

When it got dark, he walked along the highway to the bowling alley, sat down in the woods with a bottle of whiskey he stole from the old man's liquor cabinet, and waited.

Chapter Twenty

Day three without the hooch. Eddie spent most of the last two days inside his apartment, except for one trip to the market. He watched old movies, washed his sweaty sheets and pillow cases, cleaned his bathroom, slept twelve to fourteen hours each day, and didn't watch the news or read the paper. When Gwen called early in the morning, she was the first person he'd spoken to in over fifty hours.

By the time he got to her apartment, the rain was falling like an open faucet. Eddie pushed her quickly to the car, her purple raincoat pulled over her head. The water was running down Shirley Ave like a small river. Gwen hopped into the passenger seat, and Eddie folded the chair and slid it into the back. The routine was efficient. They made a good team.

Gwen was brushing the wet off her hair when Eddie started the car. "Time to build an arc," he said.

"I'm thinking you wouldn't pass for Noah," she told him.

He pulled into the slight traffic, the rain pounding the windshield.

"What's on the menu?" she asked him.

"Brattle Theater," he told her. "Double feature." Every few weeks they went to the movies. Gwen often left it up to him to decide what to see and where. She liked the surprise. Eddie loved the old theaters, second run houses trying to survive in the emerging home video craze.

"Who?" she asked.

"Hitchcock."

She wiped a space clear on the windshield with her hand.

"Psycho and Rear Window," Eddie said.

She looked at him. "You got a good night's sleep."

"You can tell?"

"I can tell."

"How?"

"I can tell," she said.

A truck passed through a giant puddle and covered the windshield with water. Gwen jumped back instinctively from the splash. "Shit," she said, "like the car wash."

The driver side wiper stopped working. Eddie jiggled the wiper button and it started again. "The touch," he said.

They drove over the Bunker Hill Bridge, sat in a bit of traffic that always gathered at the light by the Science Museum, but made good time along the river, dotted with empty sailboats, the rain dancing on the flat surface around them.

At the Brattle, Gwen wheeled herself to the front row, and parked in the aisle. Eddie sat next to her in the first seat, a large popcorn and a soda with two straws.

Once watching the Godfather here, she held his hand during the horse head scene and kept holding it for fifteen minutes, even though she'd seen it before. Eddie wanted her to hold it now, not because he wanted her to love him, but because she made him feel safe, and this clear head shit was starting to make him nervous.

In the movie *Psycho*, Janet Leigh steals some money and ends up at a seedy motel where she gets stabbed in the famous shower scene. It's clear in the beginning it's not going to end well. Eddie thought he heard Gwen whisper, "stupid bitch," before she crunched on some popcorn.

After four hours of Hitchcock, they went to Casablanca, a restaurant and café adjacent to the theater, and sat at a table next to a long mahogany bar. A movie mural, with Humphrey Bogart, Claude Rains, and Ingrid Bergman ran around the wall of the room. The place was quiet, only a few other people paired off at tables, talking over wine goblets and white coffee cups.

They ordered burgers and tea.

"I never relate to the characters in his movies. Too over the top for me," Gwen said. "Too dramatic." She cut her burger with a knife.

"Isn't that what makes a good movie, drama?" he asked.

"Not too much of it."

A tomato dropped onto her plate as she took a bite.

"You destroy a good sandwich, you know that?" he said.

"I know. I'm a pig," she answered, wiping a spot of ketchup off her chin.

"So you need to relate to every character in a film to enjoy it?"

"Not to just enjoy it, but to like it. There's a difference."

"The second one, the guy's in a wheelchair. You can't relate to that?"

"It's not so much him; it's the killer. He's a clumsy goof."

Eddie took a bite of his burger, sipped some tea, then asked, "Have you ever liked a movie where you couldn't relate?"

"No."

"Star Wars?"

"I liked it."

"Who can you relate to in that?"

She dipped a fry in ketchup, bit it halfway down. "Chewbacca."

Eddie looked at her in disbelief.

"Loyal, misunderstood," she said.

"Six-five and hairy?"

"Ever see these legs when I haven't shaved!?"

Eddie laughed over his burger. "You win," he said. "I can't argue with a chick in a wheelchair."

"Eat me," she said, and they laughed together.

Back at the apartment, Eddie pushed the chair through the doorway, hit the light switch on the way in, and then handed Gwen a small towel from the kitchen counter. "What a gentleman," she said.

"Home sweet home." He slumped on the couch.

"What now, Eddie Devlin?" Gwen asked.

"Now?"

"Now that you're a free man. Is it movies and lunch for life?"

He sat up straight. "I don't see it as freedom."

"No…Read the papers lately?"

"Not if I can help it," he said.

"They found another body in the marsh," she said, drying her hair with the towel.

He stared. "So?"

"They don't have a suspect yet."

"What are you asking, Gwen?"

"Are they going to ask you about it?"

"Why would they?"

"Why wouldn't they? You have history, right? And you've been hanging there enough."

"Not to kill someone." He walked to the kitchen and pulled a glass from the cabinet, filled it with tap water.

She kept looking. "I hope they leave you out of it."

He drank the glass empty. "Me too," he said.

"Are you okay?" she asked.

"Right as rain," he answered.

"What are you going to do?"

"I'm going to stab myself in the shower."

"I mean it."

He leaned over and kissed her on top of the head. "I'll call you in a few days," he said and quietly shut the door behind him on his way out.

Chapter Twenty-One

The Legion Highway ran past Chelsea from the Tobin Bridge in Boston, then split Revere in two, the uptown neighborhoods on one side, the streets leading to the ocean on the other. Before the exit for the beach, a stone's throw from the paddocks of Suffolk Downs, was the Turfside Diner, the morning respite for the horse track crowd. You could smell the horseshit from the stables in the parking lot. Guys came in early every day to trade tips for the afternoon, read the racebook to each other, share their 'almost' stories from the day before. It also functioned as a bank of sorts. People came to borrow or to shark money at dangerous rates.

The crowd was slight this time of day, a few stable boys and an old-timer who swept the place for breakfast and lunch. Fran, the owner, and cook, a tall, pale guy, had been on both sides of the lending business, depending on the week. When his wife died, he hit the races hard and like the locals were prone to say *some days chicken, some days feathers.*

Eddie sat at the counter, red padded stools on either side of him, stainless everywhere, three eggs, and four slices of bacon in front of him. He was thinking more about food lately since he put a cork in it. "One hot cake," he said, holding up a finger. "Just one."

"Watching your girlish figure?" Fran asked and poured a stream of batter into a perfect circle on the grill.

Eddie finished his eggs, wiped them clean with his last piece of white toast. Fran took his plate and refilled his coffee.

"Running into you all over the place," Dana said, slapping Eddie's back then taking off his brown suit jacket, hanging it on a hook attached to the booth behind them. He planted on the stool next to him.

"How many of those jackets do you own?" Eddie asked.

"Six," Dana said. "Every day but Sunday."

"What happens on Sunday?"

"Nothing but the birthday suit."

"Please," Eddie said. "I'm eating here."

The door opened and a couple of jockeys took a booth at the end of the diner car.

"Well, you're a popular guy," Dana said. "People are asking for you at the bar."

"What people?"

"Ex badge, I think. Short do, walks with a limp."

Eddie knew. "What did he say?"

"Asked if you'd been around. Were you there a couple of nights before."

"What did you tell him?"

"I told him to go fuck himself."

"And?"

"I'm not sure, but by the way he walked, it might not have been the first time."

Eddie laughed at this, but it felt a little like whistling in the dark.

"Ex-cop, right? Fisher?" Dana asked.

"Who don't you know?"

Dana smiled and nodded.

"He's an old nightmare," Eddie said, "crawling out of the woodwork."

"Speaking of old nightmares."

"I know. They should pave over that fucking marsh."

Fran slid the pancake over, and Dana looked at it. "How come his are always bigger?"

"Cause I'm not a fat bastard," Eddie said.

"Give it time, my friend," Dana told him. "I'll take three of those Fran and coffee."

Dana turned back to Eddie. "Why they so interested in you?"

"They're shooting in the dark. It's the marsh shit got them all cuckoo," Eddie answered.

"Weird," Dana said.

Fran put a coffee in front of Dana. He sipped it right away.

Eddie attacked the pancake, made it disappear in a few takes.

"Let me know if I can help," Dana said. "I'm not a total stranger in this town."

"Do I want to know who you know?"

"I know you, don't I?"

"See what I mean?" He threw some bills on the counter. Fran came by and scooped them. "I got his too," Eddie said. "Mark it down."

Dana smiled with a mouth full of pancake. "Thanks, Detective," he mumbled,

"Eddie."

"Right."

He started toward the door and stopped. "One thing."

Dana held a fork full in the air, waiting. "Name it."

"Keep the cot open."

"Consider it reserved," Dana said.

Chapter Twenty-Two

The initial sense of ease from the first few days sober, knowing what he did, no hangovers, had started to be replaced with a feeling of dread like he was not right in his own skin. And then came the jitters and more nightmares, vivid and strange, and each morning they clung to him like a shade.

He stood looking into the mirror, spreading the shaving cream onto his cheeks, remembering bits of the last dream, the beast staring at him, moving past, close enough to touch, but Eddie's arms were made of sand and he couldn't lift them. The beast snickered and ran away.

When he pressed the razor too hard it nicked his skin, and a spot of blood grew beneath the shaving cream. He splashed cold water on his face, stared at himself again, holding back the urge to cry, or scream, or punch his way through the glass. Maybe he could pull something out, something that could explain the feeling that was growing stronger with each day— the idea that he was responsible and that he could have stopped something before it all got started.

He went down for the daily double, hit for four hundred and twenty dollars, stayed five more races, and gave half of it back before circling the Marsh Road. The misery that was the race track had him thinking long and hard about a drink, about anything to kill this new pain.

The marsh was still crowded with cruisers and television vans since the recent murder, so he parked a few hundred yards away where the beaten path of stomped swamp grass wound its way back to Oak Island.

Pregnant clouds were gathering in the sky over the highway beyond, gray with black edges. The air was like a steam room. He lit a cigarette, just inside the soft turf, and walked the familiar route of the crime scene in his mind: All of them buzzing around, cops trying to move reporters, forensic guys weaving in and around the uniforms and the tape, some of the detectives making bad jokes. They were all huddled close to the river.

Then he imagined a body floating by them, near the mud-caked bank, or a piece of a body from years ago, or a head reanimated. Maybe one of the cops picked it up and tossed it back, "wrong guy," and the head screamed when it hit the water, bobbing and cursing, the words muffled by the liquid dirt filling its mouth, or maybe it just floated by unnoticed. He knew what they must be saying, the news, the brass, most of them giving the same account, no witness, no prints. Always what the marsh gives up: Nothing.

Within seconds he was surrounded by the high marsh cattails moving back and forth in the oncoming wind, looking over at Oak Island. "More fucking rain?" he whispered.

Something caught his eye, shining on the wet ground. He bent down and scooped it out of the stringy grass. It was a round coin, the size of a half-dollar, brass with a triangle logo on it, a pyramid with the number twelve inside it. He flipped it over. The words *one day at a time* were scribed on the back.

The rain came suddenly as if a bucket tipped in the sky. He hustled back to his car, skipping over the instant puddles, with the coin in his hand, knowing there was someone he needed to see.

If he hadn't been ducking the weather, he might have noticed the brown four-door Buick parked across the road a few hundred yards away. Ron Fisher was sitting just inside the open window, a pair of binoculars tight to his face.

Chapter Twenty-Three

The traffic on Revere Street moved steadily past the front of St. Theresa's church. Eddie stood outside the foyer listening to the horns honking, someone yelling from a backyard and a muffled *Led Zeppelin* song from an open window nearby— *Communication Breakdown*. He took a few more steps through the second set of freshly stained doors, and it all got quiet, like being underwater— the darkness of the dimly lit church, the dull wooden pews, the streams of light through the rose-colored windows.

He could count the times on one hand in the past twenty-five years he'd been in a church. But religion was no joke with Eddie; he honestly figured he was fucked at the end of the road, everything from whacking off too much to lifting ten bucks from his mother's pocketbook. "God," he often said, "has a good memory."

The soft red carpet felt like crossing a frozen creek. Three or four rows from the front, he genuflected, knelt on the padded riser and blessed himself like the old altar boy he was, slowly, connecting the string. There's plenty to pray for: a winning lottery number, a reinstatement, a lost body in a red flannel shirt floating to the top of the marsh, but he didn't bother, he just sat back and enjoyed the silence.

A man crossed the altar and lit a tall candle, genuflected, then lit another one. Eddie recognized his gate, his big shoulders— Joe Stang. The last time he spoke to him was Eddie's father's funeral. At the reception, Stang shook his hand with a grip that could break a bone. "If you ever need anything, look me up," he said. "I'm always in the church." He'd pointed over his shoulder toward the end of the beach. "St. Theresa's."

Eddie conjured up what he knew about him: twenty years walking the beat, then playing bodyguard for a few politicians and then the private protection racket a few months after Eddie got started. Word was Stang hit the sauce hard early in his life, then went straight and took to helping other booze hounds get off it, maybe even helping Eddie's father do the same.

The only time Eddie saw him in the station was when he came to see Preston to hawk for the church charity. He was old now, probably seventy-five, had big hands and arms, and even though he slouched, still looked like he could rip the yellow pages in half.

He walked down the aisle after tending to the altar.

Eddie stopped him. "Hi, Joe."

Stang looked at him through thick black glasses, took a second to get it together, then smiled. "Devlin?" he said.

"Got a minute."

He followed him up two flights above a barroom called Reardon's, just around the corner from the church.

"I've lived here for years," Stang said. "The rent stays cheap, and the boozehounds don't bother me anymore." They passed a red doorway and heard a conversation in Vietnamese, a slight trace of classical music. When he opened the door to his apartment, it smelled like a stale Parodi cigar, as if he'd left one smoldering in an ashtray somewhere. The walls were mostly bare, a calendar with dogs on it and a crucifix. There was a wooden coat rack with jackets and caps behind a couch covered in a green sleeve. A small television sat on a stained pine coffee table next to a bookshelf stuffed with paperbacks and VHS tapes.

Stang came back from the kitchen with half of a black tar cigar tucked into the corner of his mouth. Eddie wondered if he smoked them or just chewed them all day like some old Italian guys he used to see at the park by the high school playing bocce. He had two mugs in his hands, which he set on the coffee table. "Fresh pot," he said and sat on the green covered couch. "Still hot."

Eddie put the AA coin on the table. Stang picked it up and

looked at it. "Twelve years. It ain't yours, is it?"

"Why not?" Eddie answered quickly.

"Cause you wouldn't be here." Their eyes locked for a moment. "Some things I know."

"Maybe it's a sign?" Eddie said. "I found it today after a few days..." he hesitated, "without a drink."

"Could be," Stang said, then sipped his coffee. "They're all around us."

"I found it in the marsh," Eddie said.

"The marsh... when?"

"Earlier today."

Stang looked a little surprised, took another sip. "Pretty crowded down there, I heard. What brought you there?"

Eddie ignored the question. Another thought came to him. His mind was racing now, his nerves jumping. *What the fuck was he doing here?* "I remember you at my father's funeral," he said. "You told me if I ever needed anything to come by?"

"I did."

"I know you helped guys get sober."

"And."

"Know any with twelve years that might be hanging around the marsh?"

"Even if I did, it's an anonymous program, Eddie."

"I'll take that as a yes."

"Take it any way you want. What the heck were you doing in the marsh today?" Stang didn't want the question to get lost again.

Eddie sipped his coffee, almost threw back a mouthful. "Shit."

"Ain't it special?" Stang asked.

"Anyone on the force?" Eddie said. *Fishing for what?*

"Let's talk about you."

"I'm fine."

"You're sober. You came here. Damn right, you're fine."

Eddie stood and walked to the window, looked down over the sidewalk outside. He felt dizzy. A few guys were smoking a joint by the door of the barroom. One of them started laughing.

"Two end up dead in the marsh less than two weeks after they cut me loose."

"Go figure," Stang said.

"And then, I find that." He pointed to the coin. "And my first thought is you."

"I'm not following."

"I'm not sure there *is* anything to follow," Eddie said, turning back.

Stang puffed a little smoke from the almost dead stogie. The slight cloud seemed to hover over him like an aura.

"I'm probably just crazy, trying to make two and two out of five."

"The first few weeks are the toughest," Stang said. "Nothing makes sense."

"I suppose," Eddie said.

Another thought. "Did you help my father? Was he on it heavy?"

"That's what this is all about, your old man?"

Eddie didn't answer; the thoughts were racing again.

"We were friends," Stang said. "We helped each other." He tapped the butt of the cigar into the ashtray. "Now, what are we going to do to keep you sober?"

"We?" More dizziness.

"Oh, let me guess. You can do it on your own."

Eddie didn't say anything. He closed his hands together to stop his fingers from shaking.

"Your father would be happy you came to see me."

"I hope so," Eddie said. He looked around the apartment, the low light coming from the dark kitchen. *Like a cave.* "I'll be back if I need it."

"I'll be here," Stang told him. "In the meantime, St. Rose. Meeting every morning, eight o'clock. Can't hurt."

Eddie walked out the door, down the dimly lit stairway to the street. He was unsteady by the time he made it to his car, anxious and light-headed. *Why had he come here?*

"Something's not right," he said when he got behind the wheel. He could feel it in his spine.

He imagined Stang back in the apartment, holding the

brass coin in his hand, running his fingers over the raised inscription, a faint trace of smoke hanging the air, whispering, "Cronus."

"Shit, I need a drink," he said.

Chapter Twenty-Four

There were boxes of unsolved case files in the basement of The Revere Police Department. Most of them were from bodies that never got attached to a conviction or even a suspect. With Revere's history of wise guys, it wasn't a surprise that people ended up that way, dead and alone, without a trial following them to the newspaper. Some guys did this sort of thing for a living. They were good at it. They did it quickly and efficiently and got out of town unnoticed or came from out of town in the first place. Over the years these bodies got dumped into restaurant trash bins, or left in the trunk of a car, but more often than not, they ended up in the marsh.

But there were other boxes too: people gone missing, presumed dead, but never found. Some detectives called them 'ghosts' because they lingered in the station in that neverland, like purgatory, floating between filing cabinets, between missing and murdered. These were the ones the kids told stories about on hot summer nights smoking weed under Dizzy Bridge, the ones they figured, who ended up deep in the marsh, moving along the slippery, unreachable floor. The more the missing stayed missing in this city, the more people figured they were lying in a muddy grave a mile from the beach.

At one time, the missing names went to Ron Fisher, when he took the desk duty after a shooting, and Melvin Gillis, a cop riding out his last few years before retirement. They worked a sort of hodge-podge missing persons / cold case department. It was most likely Fisher's decision to pursue cases after a few weeks or to file them as 'still missing' or 'assumed deceased'. It didn't mean they didn't keep track of any phone records or credit card alerts, but the emphasis turned away from solving them. It was an old school way of determining whether to waste manpower on people who did not want to be found but were alive or to keep from looking for bodies that were never going to turn up.

Fisher was good at what he did; he was organized when he ran the desk, always kept a close eye on things, and with time, became adept at quietly determining what cases to pursue and what cases to let go. This sort of informed judgment had led Preston to trust Fisher to find any connection to Eddie Devlin and the recent marsh murders.

Preston stood on the first step of the bandstand pavilion, about halfway to the Point of Pines, across from a burned-out arcade building. His white shirt was damp from the moist air hanging over everything. He looked tired and hot as he scanned the boulevard, and climbed the remaining steps to the top of the pavilion. Ron Fisher was already there, sitting with his legs crossed, running shoes and sweats, a baseball cap and dark glasses. Preston sat next to him, looked out to a tanker crawling over the horizon.

"Well?" Preston asked.

"He's a loner. Hangs at the track. Has no real friends."

"Tell me something I don't know."

"The other day guess who was in the marsh looking at the crime scene from a distance."

"Revisiting?"

"Why else?"

Preston took a deep breath. "Still, it's a long shot."

"He fits the profile, Lieutenant. I'm not saying to drag him into the box yet, but now he's as good as anything you've got."

"Convince me."

"Guys like this, sometimes they split." He held his hands together, then pulled them apart. "One who does the crime, one who tries to solve it."

Preston got a chill, the idea that Eddie Devlin could be looking for suspects for the murders he committed.

"Keep on it," Preston said.

They talked a little longer and Fisher agreed to do it Preston's way. *Quietly*. Preston couldn't shake the strangeness of it all, like some late-night movie you watch with half an eye open. He looked once more at the ocean, imagining himself floating on a raft over the horizon, nothing but blue water and sunshine for as far as he could see.

Chapter Twenty-Five
The Beast

Elvin Mitchell had just finished his breakfast at home, a few scrambled eggs and a slice of cantaloupe his wife cut up the night before and left in the fridge, when his boss phoned him and asked him to come to the bowling alley. Being one of four cops in Twin Mountain, Elvin was accustomed to being on call, even if he had worked until midnight manning the phone at the station. It had been slow, just two calls, one about missing trash cans and another about a moose hit by a truck on the way up the Notch. He was awake anyway, already two cups of coffee down. The work he planned on catching up on, a few broken porch floorboards and a leaky skylight, would have to wait.

"What's up, Bud?" Elvin asked his boss, as he pulled into the bowling alley parking lot.

"It ain't pretty," Bud said. The State troopers were already walking around with their dark glasses and their chests out. They were taping off the field behind the white wooden building.

Bud leaned into the window. "As if this isn't bad enough, we got another call from a duplex on 301. A young girl, the same way."

"What way?" Elvin asked.

Bud stood back, pushed his hat up from his forehead, let the strings of white hair show on the sides. "Over there, a local kid named Murry. Sliced open from behind." He looked away as if he was going to be sick. "I bet it took him fifteen minutes to die."

He was right about the girl, also found in the woods, not far from Murry's apartment building. "She's cut up pretty good, stomach and neck," Bud told him. "Whoever it was, took their time."

Elvin knew they'd have a hard time finding a killer. People lurked all over the place up here, hikers, hunters, you never knew who was in town or out, or where anybody really came from. That was the helpless truth, when it came to crazy shit like this.

Later, when making out a report, they talked about it over coffee in the three-room police station. "The killer must have waited by this Murry's apartment, knowing the girl would come by," Bud said. "Size tens all around the scene, army boots, same as the bowling alley. Looks like a man by the shoe size."

Elvin shuffled some papers. "The guy got it first, then the girl, about an hour apart. By the time he got to her he was crazed. Real psycho."

"You can bet one thing," Bud told him, pouring more coffee into their cups. "He ain't done."

Chapter Twenty-Six

Eddie smoked another cigarette, the third in the last ten minutes, as he walked back and forth in front of St. Rose Church in Chelsea, the belly of the Tobin Bridge looming overhead. After visiting Stang, he had called the AA hotline. The person on the phone told him *8:00 sharp.*

He'd been to an AA meeting once years ago after he'd gotten drunk and fell coming into his apartment. The hospital called Eddie's father to give him a ride home. He remembered it was early in the morning, and he was maybe still drunk from the night before. His father pulled the car over to the curb at the end of Broadway, Chelsea, just before the bridge into Boston. Eddie looked up at the green steel girders, the traffic bouncing overhead, asked his father, "What's here?"

"Come with me," his father said, and the two of them walked into the basement of a brick church. Twenty or so people sat in folding chairs, most of them smoking, and one person, a young guy, Eddie's age, was talking from a podium facing the crowd. He joked about being drunk and thinking he was Don Juan, recounting how he puked on his shoes when he and his date were about to make out. "That's how sexy booze made me," he said.

That was about all Eddie could remember from that one meeting, that and a few guys shaking his hand (which made him uncomfortable) and his father talking to a big guy stacking chairs afterward.

He realized now it must have been Stang.

Eddie's father didn't lecture him after the meeting, didn't go on about the dangers of alcohol. Those talks were over.

When he got back to Eddie's apartment, they both sat with

the car idling while Eddie got himself together and opened the door. Just before he stepped out onto the sidewalk his father said, "don't drink and drive, Eddie. At least that's one way you won't die."

Eddie never went back to AA. But he was no stranger to drunks. About a year after he'd been on the force, he'd taken a part-time job as a bartender, one night a week, at a regulars 'no tell' tavern in the basement of a restaurant on the beach. It was at the end of the strip. It got some transient beach people, but not many, mostly folks who didn't want the traffic, or having to deal with the bikers or the punks. It was a safe place, the drinks were cheap, and the people behaved. He stood behind the glass-front crescent bar, poured drinks, made small talk with the regulars.

One night he listened to a guy going on about his girlfriend, the one his wife didn't know about, how she screwed him, spent his money and left him for another guy. "A fucking spic waiter. You believe that?" he said to Eddie. "I know where she went though. I'll fix her ass."

The guy was short, thick fingers wrapped around a rocks glass full of whiskey.

Later, as he paid his check, the guy said, "If you ever need a roof or a siding job, give me a call. Name is Steve Salvi."

"Officer Devlin," Eddie said. The guy's face went blank for a second. He dropped a twenty on the bar and walked out. Eddie watched the square construction shoulders turning through the narrow doorway, whispered, "Scumbag," tossing the dirty glass into the sink.

He crushed another cigarette to the sidewalk and looked up at the statue of the Virgin Mary over the doorway of St. Rose church. He wanted to believe this was the same church his father brought him to twenty years ago, and that this moment was serendipitous, but the truth was he couldn't remember, and there had to be five churches up and down this street. Eddie loved his father, and right now he wished he could tell him, put his arm around his shoulder and let him know he was sorry for all the crazy shit, wished he had been with him in Florida when he died, wished he could blink his eyes and be twelve-years-old at Fenway Park, his father handing him a hot dog and smiling down to him, rubbing his head. "How's this, squirt?"

"This is great, Dad."

He walked a few hundred yards in each direction, then stopped, watched a few guys in jean jackets jog down the stairs to the basement of the church. One of them was laughing. *What could be so funny?* Eddie thought, before he headed back down Broadway to his car.

Chapter Twenty-Seven

The weathermen were trying to save face again, turning away from their previous predictions and playing excited that records could be broken if the rain kept up. It had already been coming down off and on for ten days. The sewers ran over, most of the streets flooded. It felt like the marsh was creeping back to the ocean and clawing at everything in between.

Roman was sitting behind a paper-stacked desk in his junkyard office, a poster of a naked girl stretched out on a Harley Davidson on the wall behind him, the rain tapping fast on the tin roof of the trailer. He kicked his cowboy boots up on the corner, dragged on a cigarette. The phone rang and he answered it on the second ring.

"Ya...Let me guess...Is that what you call it these days?" He laughed, then listened, his face suddenly focused. "Ya, ya," he said, "I forgot to tow it. I must have been fucked up. Sue me." He listened again. "Really," he said. "Next time find someone else to clean up your shit."

He slammed the phone down. "Asshole," he said.

Chapter Twenty-Eight

"Koslowski?" Gwen asked.

"The Polish Hitchcock," Eddie said, "but much more philosophical." He was leaning in behind her antique-looking television set.

Gwen scooted out of her chair to the couch, smoothed the front of her long white dress.

Eddie put the video in the player he had rigged up on the floor next to it.

"Is that even going to work?" she asked.

"I think so," he said. "I *was* the self-appointed video tech at the station, you know." He joined her on the couch, and took the bowl of popcorn from the table, put it between them.

"What's this one again?"

Eddie spoke with a mouthful, "Camera Buff."

He jumped up and shut the light. The deep violin music played over the credits, the tiny set flashed in the darkness over their faces, their hands dipping to the white plastic bowl and up to their mouths.

"You're not drinking these days," Gwen said, keeping her eyes on the screen.

"Neither are you," Eddie answered.

And the movie took over, the thick polish accents, the sound of traffic and the city. The tiny apartment filled with the single speaker sound of men talking and the quiet munching of popcorn.

Ninety-eight minutes later, the white bowl lay empty on the beige carpet. Gwen was leaning slightly closer to Eddie, the last bit of violin strings fading, the flashing light turning to snow. Eddie got up and turned the set off. "Good to know you can watch a VHS, become part of the twentieth century."

"I like the movie house better."

"Me too," he said, putting the tape back in the box. "I can rent more from him."

"Not too soon," Gwen said. "He's depressing, even for me."

"But true, don't you think?"

"It makes me want to watch Singing in the Rain or White Christmas."

"White Christmas is a subversive white supremacist movie."

"But I like the music," she said.

Eddie took the bowl to the kitchen, rinsed it out in the sink, and started drying it with a dishtowel. His hands shook a little, but better than the day before. "I have something I want to talk to you about and you have to promise not to say I'm crazy."

"Promise." Gwen adjusted herself on the couch.

"You'd say that anyway, just to hear."

"Cross my heart." She made the motion over her breast with her fingers.

Eddie dried his hands with the towel and sat on the edge of the couch, keeping a little distance.

"A year after the body disappears, two more get killed and dumped in the marsh."

"Ya," Gwen said.

"I think there's something to it, something that wants to point to me."

"You're crazy."

"You said..."

"Just kidding. Go on."

"I'm there every other day."

"That much?"

"You knew I was there a lot, Gwen, come on."

"So, you go to the marsh."

"Two bodies turn up *in the marsh*. I get fired, I'm..." he stopped to think of a way to say it, "not exactly conducting myself in a responsible manner, and I'm haunted by this ..."

"What are you saying?"

"I don't know. I stop drinking for two weeks and then I find this gold AA coin there and that leads me to think about a guy my father knew, an ex-cop, so I go see him."

"To get help?" she asks.

"Maybe. But when I get there, I start asking him about people he knows who might go to the marsh. I'm playing cop again, right, and something about it, something about him, gave me the creeps, and then I think none of this makes sense."

Gwen straightened her back.

Eddie could feel himself getting dizzy again. "What if someone is using this?"

"I don't get it, Eddie. For what?"

"To make it look like me, and then soon they'll come looking to do more than just talk."

Eddie circled to the kitchen, tossed the towel in the sink. "And the worst part is, I spend my time driving around, watching television. Outside of seeing you and being at the track, I have nowhere to be."

"Aren't you jumping ahead a little? Are you worried about an alibi?"

"Someone came to see Dana, another ex-cop I know. He was asking questions."

"What kind of questions?"

"The kind they ask when they want to pin something on someone. Trust me, Gwen. The things this guy investigates are strictly off book." He was almost out of breath.

Gwen sat back, brushed a hand through her hair. "What do you do?"

"I think I do some investigating of my own."

"And me?" Gwen asked.

"What do you mean?"

"You don't expect me to sit around and let you botch the fucking thing, do you?"

"You have to sit, Gwen. You have no choice."

"Fuck you, Eddie. Tell me. What do you see in that marsh?" she asked. "Why do you keep going there?"

His hands shook. He got dizzy again. *I could have stopped*

it. And he saw them, the beast, himself, the girl, all of them in some freaky circle dance, holding hands over the marsh, around and around and around.

"Better still," Gwen said. "Why don't you show me?"

Chapter Twenty-Nine

The rain hit the windshield in a steady rhythm, thick fat drops against the dark night ahead. They drove silently, everything floating around in Eddie's head: *Why give someone a view of your darkest places?* Or maybe that wasn't it; maybe he was just pulling Gwen into something where she didn't belong. He always felt like he'd protected her by not getting too close, too intimate, but things were changing. It could be the days without the sauce or seeing more of her since the force cut him loose, but he felt the overwhelming urge to tell her that this could work between them. He would. When they got back to the apartment, he would help her off with her coat, make some tea, and sit on the couch next to her and say it. He would say, "I love you, Gwen."

"I'm still not sure this is a good idea," Eddie said.

"I want to know," she said. "I want to know everything if I'm going to help you."

So he told her everything.

He told her what he'd been doing, what he'd been thinking, all the crazy irrational fears he kept locked away, the coin, Stang, the junkyard, the marsh mornings, the dreams and the guilt. She asked questions about that night over a year ago, what he expected to find standing in the marsh day after day, or in the junkyard, why he thought the coin wasn't just something someone dropped a long time ago. He did his best to answer, to revisit some of his thinking, but he didn't really know himself. Everything with him was a hunch, a feeling, and he wasn't sure if those mechanisms were working for him or against him. Telling her might have been cathartic in one way, but hearing himself talk about it made him think he was just crazy, trying to fit together the random pieces of a puzzle he was inventing on the fly.

The tires crunched on the gravel shoulder, and the headlights lit up the tall weeds, eerily still this windless night. The rain was suddenly more of a drizzle. Eddie opened the passenger side door and set up the chair for her. He moved her into the seat and turned toward the darkness. They would walk through this together. She would get him to forget. And he would protect her.

He moved her along the rocky, gravel edge by the dirty water, shined a flashlight into the marsh, and pushed her further on a stretch of hard turf. When they stopped, he walked a little ahead of her. "I found the coin over there," he said and pointed to his right. "Closer to Oak Island."

Gwen looked that way and back, her eyes squinting to see. "It's spooky here at night," she said.

"It's spooky anytime," Eddie said, his back to her, looking over the sea of wild swamp. They stayed silent for a few seconds.

He looked deeper into the marsh like he was looking into his soul, all the fear, all the dark places he'd been, all the secrets and the scum stacked like car bodies in the junkyard.

"Am I crazy?" he asked, turning around.

"No more than the rest of us," she said.

He walked closer to her. "I'm chasing a ghost aren't I?"

"We all have them, Eddie. Maybe yours is already dead somewhere out there." She pointed to the marsh. "Maybe that's where your search is going to end, right where it started."

Where it started. The phrase made him freeze. He looked to his right, toward the faded lights of Oak Island, took a few steps in that direction and stopped as if he was facing a wall. "It started there," he said and remembered how he had looked into the marsh, the cattails swaying and their eyes, face to face, like a magician showing you the hole in that hat, *can't you see stupid, it's a trick,* and he could see the dreams were not just dreams, the girl that got raped, before Cronus was born.

"I was there that night," he said. "It was him."

"Who?" Gwen asked.

"The beast," he whispered to himself, and panic ran up his spine, the chill making his body shake.

"We got called to the Island for a sexual assault. He was standing in front of me." His hands shook. "And I passed out."

"Who was standing in front of you?" Gwen asked.

Eddie stared at her. The ghost was real. "He came back."

She held out her hand, and he took it, knelt on one knee by the chair.

"Who was it, Eddie?" she asked.

He closed his eyes and fought off the dizziness. "I let him go," he whispered.

It felt like the marsh was about to close in around him, the weeds moving inch by inch to take him, the marsh sounds deafening: the insects, the water running, the wind, the bodies sliding beneath his feet. He looked up at her. "And the rest of it," he said. "That's invented? The people out to get me?"

"We do what we have to do. It's okay. I'm here to help."

He felt the tears filling his eyes. "My hell, Gwen. It haunts me every fucking minute, and now... how do I let that go?"

"We're human, Eddie," she said. "Sometimes the best we can do is to move on."

She squeezed his hand. "Close your eyes." He did, and she said it. "The demon is dead."

"The demon is dead," he said. But he didn't believe it. He kept his eyes closed tight, let himself get lost in the words they repeated to each other, "the demon is dead." The black marsh night hung around them, the rain, the trembling, the silence.

When he opened his eyes, Gwen was staring at him. How long had it been? Minutes? Hours? "Let's go home," she said. "We'll figure this out together."

She smiled and put a hand on his arm. He turned her toward the road and pushed her chair over the soft turf. The rain got heavier, quickly, thick cold drops, soaking the earth around them. By the time they got to the car, the wheels of the chair were caked with mud. He would clean them when they got back, take a rag and wipe down the chair like a teenager with his new bike.

He was reaching for the passenger door when he heard it — far away at first, like someone revving an engine on the highway across the marsh, maybe a biker shifting into the passing lane, heading up Route One, but he realized almost immediately that it was closer, the headlights maybe fifty yards away.

The high beams flicked on and off, blinding them for a second. A truck, Eddie thought, by the height of the lights. Gwen looked into the glare and Eddie pulled her chair back toward the marsh, but the wheels sank a few inches in the mud. He tugged again but lost his footing, felt his hands slipping from the slick grips of the chair. Gwen yelled, "Eddie," and he turned toward the lights...

The truck slammed into the bumper of Eddie's car and pushed it through the gravel shoulder, the metal creasing instantly, a spark of red, the truck engine turning gears. The speed of the collision flipped the car into the first layer of wetland. As it rolled onto the roof, it pinned Gwen and her chair beneath it. Eddie reached for her, the left front fender pressing into the side of his head and driving him into the mud. He lay there barely conscious, trying to breathe through the rotting sludge. "Gwen," he said, and he heard the truck rev its engine, and he knew before he blacked out that it was coming to ram them again.

Part Two - The Return

"Here's the exit, your way out.
Here's the world with no one in it."

— January O'Neil

Chapter Thirty

When winter approached, the beach shed its skin and turned a muted gray from sand to sky. The cold water that had been seaweed stricken over the summer got bluer with the rows of small white caps rolling in. The sea wall stayed empty, except for the weekends, and the only people on the beach in the morning were the clammers at low tide or the hooded men moving in slow circles with long-handled metal detectors. The boardwalk still got some walkers in sweat suits or knit hats and mittens, and a few pockets of folks with baseball caps huddled with coffee and cigarettes under the pavilions.

Dana drove his gold Caddie slowly along the quiet boulevard. "I like this time of year on the beach," he said. "Less traffic to sit in, less time to get where you're going."

Eddie sat next to him looking out at an empty section of seawall and a gang of seagulls picking through a trash barrel. In the distance, he saw a man and his dog running between the low tide puddles and an oil tanker crawling along the horizon. Turning to see was difficult for him even though the soft collar was less restrictive than the iron-rod halo he had to wear for six weeks. The painkillers helped, but he still felt plenty of fire in every wrong move. His body reminded him often that he had a long way to go. He reached down to itch his leg that was still peeling dry skin since the cast came off a week ago. Not being too eager to get back to his apartment, Eddie relaxed into the ride, looking out the window at the treasure hunters combing the sand. "Think they ever find anything out there?" he asked.

Dana glanced from the road. "Change and keys," he said. "I knew a guy who went down twice a week in the summer.

95

Had a draw full of car keys."

"The promise but not the payoff."

"The only ones making dough are the ones selling those machines," Dana said.

Eddie almost laughed at that, but it hurt too much to laugh. He stared at the beach sky, feeling like a man who just got out of jail, and tried to piece things together. The police and the fire department were the first to find Gwen's body crushed beneath the weight of the car. Unlike her, he was still breathing somewhere under the crumpled maze of metal, his leg broken, his pelvis crushed, a ruptured cervical vertebra at the top of his spine. The impact also broke four of his ribs, caused internal bleeding and lacerations of the spleen. He stayed in a coma for two and a half weeks, and once, during that first night, he stopped breathing for ten seconds.

When he regained consciousness, they took him off the vent and moved him from intensive care. He stayed seven weeks in the hospital and two more months in a connecting rehab.

Preston came to see him when it looked like he was on the mend, told him Gwen most likely died from the initial impact and didn't suffer. Eddie found some solace in that. Preston also told him the wake and the funeral were a tribute to her work and that people she helped over the years came in big numbers to pay respect and give thanks for all she did. "As far as the investigation," he said, "we're treating it as a hit and run. No witnesses to the crash."

Eddie didn't cry when they left him alone that night; instead, he felt himself becoming dense to it all. He started to look at it methodically, without emotion. He asked later about Gwen's apartment and the things she left behind, and they told him a cousin from Vermont had cleaned it out, but they were holding a small box of things with his name on it.

"Who's holding it," Eddie asked.

"The Department," Preston told him. "Come by when you're ready."

Eddie knew what that meant, a casual way of saying, 'we've got some questions'.

Dana got to the circle at the end of the boulevard, made a U-turn, and then pulled the car over to the sidewalk. He lit a cigarette, blew some smoke out the window toward the Boston skyline. "Well?" he asked.

"Up and back one more time," Eddie said. "Then hook it over to the marsh."

Chapter Thirty-One

A few months earlier, on Halloween night, Eddie stood behind the fifth-floor window in the hospital rehab, metal rods still grounded to his shoulders, his body stiff as a three-week bender. He looked over the streets below him, the packs of goblins, fairies, and monsters cruising up and down the grid, like candy-seeking zombies. The sun had set, and the shadows played games with the flowing capes and the rubber masks, disappearing beneath the overhanging branches and behind the tall stick-built fences. Maybe because the painkillers were still flowing through his system or the way his head felt, suspended without him, unattached, or maybe not having been outside for so long, but suddenly he felt like he was flying over the rooftops, his arms outstretched, gliding in slow circles above the children, their eyes looking into the sky, some in horror, some in awe, some frozen and staring. And as he flew, the mothers grabbed their children and ran them up the front stairs of their porches, doors slamming and bolting, except for this one child, a black cape and a white painted face. He never ran, never moved, he stood straight and spread his tiny arms as wide as he could, the cape blowing in the wind. He stared back up at the flying creature, bared his long sharp teeth, and waited.

Eddie knew him. He was all kids, all tough guys, all victims, all people turned inward, facing the fear with more fear, facing the night, facing death with false courage, with a costume to hide behind. But, he knew none of it could save the one brave child from being swallowed by the hovering evil, his last thoughts of a warm living room, of his father throwing a football, of his dog climbing on his bed one dark rainy night (both afraid of the thunder). Nothing could save the brave little boy because he would always remember, and the more he tried to forget, the more it grew, circling him, closer and closer, until only darkness, and cold, and sweeping him up.

Chapter Thirty-Two
The Beast

Kyle Hardy rode the bus from Portsmouth, bound for South Station in Boston. He sat against the window, thinking of what he had done, a slight adrenaline rush rising to his head. It seemed so easy, waiting patiently with the mosquitos, sipping whiskey. Each time someone came through the door of the bowling alley, he got ready, felt the fear rising in his throat. Even then, it didn't seem real. He had been in fights, had endured his old man's beatings. He knew violence, had even killed a dog back in the marsh, then had his way with Gina back there, but this, this was new. (Yet he was sure of it.)

With each new swing of the bowling alley door, the sudden clamor of the music inside, the shaft of light falling to the parking lot, he set himself on his haunches like some wild animal he'd seen hiding in the brush of the jungle on television. It built inside him each minute, the reality of it, the excitement. He rolled the knife in his fingers, the wooden handle, the sharp curve.

Then finally, with one last swing of the door, he came out. The fucking prick. He was whistling when he walked to his car, some song from the jukebox. He fumbled in his pockets for his keys, and Kyle snuck up behind and stuck the knife in his throat and pulled back along the seam like he was cutting a square, and dragged him back into the woods. Once there, he went to work on the rest of him. He was surprised by the lack of sound, just a gurgling that eventually faded to nothing: no screaming, no real fight.

"Now who's funny," he said, plunging the blade one more time.

Then, at the apartment, he watched her unlock the door and go inside. When he knocked, she opened it, no anticipation, no fear. "Hey," she said.

He was swift. He had initially planned to do what he'd done to Gina in the marsh, but something else was ruling him now, something more urgent.

When he was done, he rubbed mud over the bloodstains and changed into the clothes in the gym bag, the red flannel shirt and jeans. He walked well into the woods, dug a shallow hole with his hands, buried the bloody clothes, then headed for the highway to hitch a ride south.

A couple of locals in a pickup truck gave him a ride down Route Sixteen. They didn't talk much, mostly listened to loud rock music and passed a joint back and forth. When they let him off about three miles from Portsmouth, the driver asked him, "Where to now, buddy?"

Kyle stood outside on the road. "I think I'll go home and kill my father," he said.

"No shit," the driver answered. "Good luck with that." And the two of them laughed and drove off.

Chapter Thirty-Three

Eddie looked out the window as if he was sightseeing, everything a little dreamy and slowed down from the painkillers. They passed the junkyard. The wooden gates that were always open were shut, and a sign read *closed* in black letters on a piece of white cardboard.

"What happened?" Eddie asked. "The scumbag retire?"

"Don't know. It's been that way for a while."

"Maybe he OD'd on his own dope and the rats took him home for the winter."

"Wishful thinking," Dana said. They made a U-turn and headed back to the southbound side of the marsh, parked right where Eddie pointed, on the familiar gravel shoulder.

"I might as well get this over with," he said and pushed the door open with his foot. He turned his body toward the marsh, sat and looked at the wind-swept weeds, the cattails browner now with the coming winter. Slowly he grabbed the top of the door frame with two hands and pulled himself to a standing position. He stood that way for a few seconds before attempting to move again. The fireworks in his muscles took a test run through his body.

Dana stood off to the side.

Eddie took a few steps on the brown straw turf, crunching under his feet, not as sponge-like as the last time he stepped foot on it. It felt like kindling waiting to ignite from a stray cigarette flicked out a car window, one of those brush fires that left a swath of charred weeds like a black tar road.

"Where's the fucking rain," Eddie whispered to himself and remembered the drops on the windshield, the puddles on the street, the steady beat of it, as if he missed it. He imagined it to be the Irish in him, always feeling a little damp or chilled, looking for a brandy and a fireplace. But then he remembered the build-up to that last night with Gwen, how the rain had been pressing on him, heavy and humid, the constant cloud draped on his shoulders.

A cold breeze hit him from across the dirty river, and for some reason, he thought about a movie he'd seen as a kid—alien beings living underground in a laboratory and people being sucked below by swirling sand pits. He'd gone out to play after watching it. The sky was dark, and the neighbor kids had written *tornado warning* on the street in chalk. Eddie had this feeling that day that he wasn't safe, that a cloud inside his body was ready to push him into a darkness he would never escape from.

Dana walked softly up behind him.

"Let's go for a drink," Eddie said, without turning around.

Chapter Thirty-Four

Jurek left Ukraine when he was seventeen, ten years before he ended up in Revere. He had a grocery list of last names (depending on his visa status), Relic, Bosh, Skelski. He spent some time in Paris as a waiter, then got a visa to work in the United States with a Marriot Hotel on the Long Wharf in Boston. That job lasted for three years. He lived in a North End Flat with three other waiters. Two of them were Czechs, the other a Russian named Dimitri, or that's what he called himself. Dimitri was tall, maybe six foot four, long brown hair. He'd played a little basketball in Europe, nothing special, travel money and enough for three meals a day. He was a friendly guy, and he was always flush. He bought Jurek lunch now and then, drinks on Causeway Street, and scalped tickets to the Celtics on occasion. The two hit it off. They talked a lot about Europe, got philosophical about the struggle disguised as *the American Dream.*

One night, walking back from the market after drinks, Dimitri, said. "I'm moving to a condo on the beach in Revere. I got a health club, pool, doorman."

"Sweet," Jurek said.

"I'm leaving the hotel too."

"For what?"

"Come by," Dimitri said. "Check it out." He handed him a plain white card with an address, no name. "I'll tell you all about it."

A week later, Jurek took the subway to Wonderland Station and walked the half-mile to the pink high-rise condo building overlooking the south end of the boulevard. He dropped Dimitri's name to the doorman, who directed him to the far set of elevators reserved for the upper level. When he got off on the top floor, Dimitri was there waiting outside the doors, a cold beer in each hand. He handed one over.

"Welcome," he said.

"Thanks," Jurek said, looking past him to the picture window, the ocean beyond and the Boston skyline. He pointed with the beer as they walked into the living room. "Nice view."

The condo was modest, wall to wall carpet, a few leather couches and a small kitchen with a wooden table and chair set. It looked new and clean.

They sat on the couch by the window. "You must have saved your tips," Jurek said.

"Another line of work came my way," Dimitri said. "But you already knew that."

Jurek sipped his beer.

He knew.

Chapter Thirty-Five

Dana left Eddie in the apartment after putting the groceries away, three bags from the deli: two frozen pizzas, some cold cuts, eggs, juice, thick-cut bacon from the deli. The last bag had two six-packs of beer and two pints of Mr. Boston vodka.

They had stopped at the track for three drinks and four races before the market. Eddie got legless suddenly at the bar, the booze and whatever else they sent him home with taking its toll. Dana had to help him to the car, the same way he'd helped many customers to a waiting taxi cab over the years, hanging their keys on a hook next to the register. He listened to him mumble something about 'Gwen', but couldn't make out the rest.

He managed to get him to the couch in his apartment, and just before he left, he stood over him for a few minutes, making sure he was still breathing, like a father over his newborn's crib. He knew Eddie Devlin had been a tortured soul for years, the drinking, the job, the marsh, everything tugging at him. Dana was not usually the sentimental type, but he wished there was something he could do to ease his friend's pain.

Eddie woke up about three hours after Dana left, his head pounding, his body one great spiking throb. He pulled himself from the couch and walked into the bedroom, where his disheveled bed lay frozen in time from three months ago. The draw of the bedside table was partially open, and he removed a yellow envelope. He withdrew the card from it and held it in his hands. The outside jacket had a picture of Alfred Hitchcock on it, the inside a hand-written note:

To my real-life Hitchcock.
Don't fall out any Rear Windows.
Happy Birthday.
Love Gwen.

He smiled once quickly, then sat on the bed, holding the card like a prayer book. Almost instantly, he was overcome with guilt. With all the mistakes of his life, he knew none were bigger than taking Gwen to the marsh that night.

He untied his high-cut sneakers, kicked them off, then reached behind and pulled the soft collar from around his neck, let it fall to the floor. When he closed his eyes and began to drift off into the drug and alcohol-induced sleep, he thought of a time when he was an altar boy and the impure thoughts he used to have during mass. God had been taking notes all along; he was sure of that.

Chapter Thirty-Six

Joe Stang swept the cement steps of St. Theresa's church, moved the broom briskly, pushing a pile of dust to the sidewalk, then into the street. He did a good job when he cleaned the church and he was proud of how he kept it. No stranger to the broom, he'd swept the floors in his father's barroom when he was a kid. After the morning sweep, he'd sit on one of the high bar stools and drink a cold coke while his father quartered a sour pickle for him from the big glass jar by the cash register. "I like having you around, kid," he'd say to him.

One morning Joe was carrying a case of beer up from the cellar when he heard voices yelling, and then a loud pop, followed by a rumble of bodies and what sounded like chairs falling. Joe stayed where he was, his hands gripping the case.

He wasn't sure how long before he walked up the stairs and found his father lying between two fallen stools, his eyes wide open and a pool of blood still oozing from a hole in his chest.

The police asked him lots of questions in the next few days— what he heard, what he'd seen. None of his answers seemed to help much.

About a week after the shooting, Joe's mother found him at the bar with a mop and a broom cleaning the floor. She let him do it every morning for the next month before they sold the place and moved to another apartment near the beach.

Joe once asked her if they ever found out who killed his father. "No," she said. "Too many dirty cracks in the city for the scum to hide."

Father Brice stepped onto the church landing, a black cassock and a silver cross on his chest. He looked at Joe through small wire-framed glasses. "Looks good, Joe," he said. "Especially the flowers on the altar."

"A new florist on Broadway," Stang said. "They called and told me they were throwing them out."

"The kindness of strangers," Brice said.

Stang smiled and made a few more broad strokes into the street.

Brice turned and went back inside the church, the tall wooden doors closing behind him with a creak.

Stang looked above the doors as they closed, noticed some caulking coming loose where the stained glass met the door frame. He made a mental note to fix it before the real cold weather came. He was walking back up the stairs when he heard his name, "Joe," almost inaudible, above the passing traffic.

Across the street from the church was a small smoke shop, *cigars, cigarettes, the lottery.* Ron Fisher stood in the alley next to it, leaning against the wall, a half-smoked cigar in his fingers.

Joe left the broom against the door of the church and crossed against the oncoming Revere Street traffic. Someone honked but he didn't pay attention.

"You sweep a mean street," Ron said, taking a drag.

"And proud of it," Joe answered. "You ought to try it someday."

"Nah. I'll leave it to the good guys." He blew on the tip of the cigar. "Your boy is home."

Stang stared back.

"But you probably know that already." He shook his head a little. "The guy is like fucking Rasputin."

"What about Preston?" Stang asked.

"He still thinks what he thinks," Ron said, "mostly what I feed him."

"He trusts you?"

Ron took a step. "Must be the baby face." He rubbed a hand over his three-day beard, and smiled.

109

"Devlin. How is he?"

"What do you expect, a fucking car sat on top of him."

"Did Preston pull you?"

"Not yet," Ron said. "Since there have been no more murders, he wants to know where he goes now that he's out."

Stang thought about that. "She was one of the good guys, you know?"

"I know," Ron answered. "But the game has changed."

"Still, we need to finish it. For her sake." He looked back at the church. "You know that stupid motherfucker told me he thought the car was empty."

"Like you said," Ron answered. "He's a stupid motherfucker."

"What goes around comes around, right?"

"Let's hope so," Ron said, and tucked the cigar in his mouth. "Otherwise we're all fucked."

Stang watched him walk away until he turned the corner toward the racetrack, then he looked across the street at the sidewalk in front of the church. It looked neat and clean; even the cracks were swept free of grass and weeds, the fall leaves brushed away— everything in order.

Chapter Thirty-Seven

After two weeks at home, Eddie slept for four hours without any pain, a new record, until he turned the wrong way, and the fire came back to his neck. He curled his way out of bed, both feet flat on the floor, and got his knees to straighten. The metal hospital cane by the side of his bed came in handy even though he hated the idea of it. He felt like the old drunk on the beach with the rummy legs, needing a push to cross the street like one of those Christmas toys that waddled down the back of a hardcover book.

His head was heavy with a familiar hangover.

When he took that first drink at the racetrack after getting out of the hospital rehab, he held the glass in his hands like a chalice. "Here's to nothing," he said, looking at the bartender, a new kid. *What did he know?* He made the sign of the cross in his mind. *Bless me, father.*

No bells or whistles, no real ceremony, just the cold, bitter beer sliding down his throat, that smell instantly on his breath.

It took him no time to get into the old swing, with the misery and the madness all around him. *Who stays sober at the racetrack?*

He walked into the kitchen, opened the cabinet doors above the white stove, a half-full box of cereal, a bottle of vodka he hadn't gotten to yet, and a loaf of white bread.

Getting used to being alone again was easy, no nurses, no physical therapists, nowhere he had to be. Dana was the only one who came to visit except for Lieutenant Preston. Eddie must have been out of it when Preston came by because he left a note in the mailbox.

Come see me when you're up to it. Al.

He poured a cup of tea, added a shot of Irish whiskey from the bottle on the counter, popped two Percocets, and washed them down with orange juice from the almost empty carton. The apartment was quiet, too quiet maybe, as he sipped his tea, waiting for the numb hush to come back. Maybe he would shower and shave and then go see Preston. *Why not?* he figured.

His muscles relaxed even more under the hot shower spray, and he felt himself slipping away with the heat and the sound of the water beating down on him. He pictured himself talking to Preston, both of them shaking hands in the marsh and Eddie pointing out the place where the beast had been. Then Preston pointing to some other spot, each of them coming up with different scenarios and digging the earth around the shallow dirty water with short shovels, the mud piling up behind them until they were hundreds of feet below the overgrowth. Then in a cave, like the one he'd seen in a movie version of a Jules Verne novel, he is pointing a flashlight to a shallow chamber, the light revealing a man, a red flannel shirt, sitting hunched and cold against the slimy rock, a slight smile on his face, and Preston handing Eddie a gun and saying, "finish it."

The water turned cold, and it brought him back and he prayed the day would come, when Preston would know something for real.

Chapter Thirty-Eight

It had been raining hard that night. The patter on the trailer roof was loud and constant. Roman stuck the bong to his lips, the blue glass tube filling with a white cloud. He sucked his cheeks hollow, then let out a breath of smoke that spread to the walls of the tiny room. After his last sip of beer, he tossed the can behind the desk in the vicinity of a trash can. It hit the floor and rolled around with the other empties.

He stood and stretched, his stomach hanging over his belt buckle, let out a burp and laughed, thinking of the girl who left an hour before, the things she did for a half a gram of cooked cocaine.

Outside he climbed into his black tow truck. A few nights a week, he would drive around the city checking for cars that looked abandoned or ones he recognized from the week before with parking tickets piled under the wiper. He towed them back and let them sit for a few weeks after going through them. If nobody came looking, he could sell them or sell the parts to the mechanics who came around on the weekends.

Even though he knew he fucked up a few nights ago when he got the call, passed out drunk, and forgot to tow the purple El Dorado from the marsh, he whispered, "Fuck him," the more he thought about it.

The streets near the beach were empty this night. Roman sparked a joint and decided to call it quits. He turned the radio up, a J. Geils song blasted, and he started singing, stomping on the floor of the truck with his free foot and driving through the circle to the Marsh Road.

A short distance from the junkyard, he noticed a car across

the divider, parked on the shoulder and heading in the opposite direction. He squinted through the rain on the windshield. A smile came to his face as he recognized the green Grand Marquis. "Devlin," he whispered. He slowed and looked again at the empty driver's side, no lights, slapped the dash hard. "Fucking A," he yelled and giggled as he punched the gas, covered the last mile and half quickly and made the U-turn at the light.

The rain picked up and he stared between the streaks of the wiper blade, the dark empty road ahead of him, just his headlights on the black tar. He was high enough to feel the adrenaline coursing through his veins.

Eddie's car was a few hundred yards away now. He slowed, flashed his high beams once on and off. The rain had gotten heavier, the blur on the windshield like stained-glass. He sped up again, pulled quickly onto the shoulder, the radio blaring, *my baby, my baby...*

He grabbed the steering wheel with both hands. "Who's the pig boy now, asshole," he yelled.

The first hard crunch bent the frame and sent the car toppling over. The impact surprised him, and he lurched forward, banging his head on the windshield. He gathered himself and jammed it in reverse and hit it again, pushed it further over the gravel and into the first layer of marsh mud.

He sped away, laughing. "Call for a tow, pig, when you get back from playing in the weeds."

Chapter Thirty-Nine

Eddie drove himself to the station in a car Dana dropped off, a dented red Mustang in need of a tune-up (it coughed in first gear). Dana told him some trucker from Canada asked if he could park it outside the bar for a few days. "After two months, I took it as a tip," he said.

It felt strange to be behind the wheel again, but Eddie liked the motion, the movement. Standing still was the hardest for him. He handled the car carefully in and out of traffic along the boulevard, parked it behind the station on Ocean Ave.

When he walked inside, a few people perked up and waved, *Hey Eddie Devlin, how's it going?* He smiled back, moving through the office maze, one guy patting him on the back just before he got to Preston's door. He knocked on the bottom of it with the tip of the cane. "Come in," he heard from the other side. Preston put a book down spine open on the desk.

"Mr. Devlin," he said, stood and extended his hand. They shook, and Eddie sat down opposite him.

"Lieutenant."

"Al, please. How are you getting on?" Preston asked.

"I'm okay," Eddie lied. He didn't tell him how his sleep was interrupted by any small movement, how he'd been living in a drug-induced haze since getting out of a coma, how his disability check was barely enough to keep him in food and rent. "Getting by," he said.

Preston pulled out a cardboard box from somewhere behind his desk. It had a sticker with a department logo on it, Eddie's name written in magic marker, *E. Devlin.* "These are the things Gwen's cousin thought you might want," Preston said.

He put it on the corner of the desk and pushed it slightly in Eddie's direction.

"What's in it?" Eddie asked.

"Personal things, memorabilia mostly. Look at it when you get home."

Eddie held the box, and it all got kind of hazy like the room was filling with fog, and for a second, he felt as if he were going to pass out.

"I have a few questions," Preston said. "Some things to clear up."

Eddie snapped to.

"Why were you and Gwen in the marsh that night?"

"That's personal."

"It's important."

He shifted in the chair, felt a twinge of pain run up his side. "Look, Lieutenant...Al," he said sarcastically. "What I was doing there had nothing to do with what happened there. She was trying to help me."

"No doubt," Preston said. "We...I just want to know in what capacity, a friend, a therapist, and why there? Why then?"

"These things you want to clear. Is one of them me?"

Preston looked at him, closed his book, and put it on the shelf behind him.

"You've been a cop a long time. You know how it works. No one is accusing you of anything."

"Not yet."

Preston turned back. He wasn't in the mood for this anymore. "Anything I can do for you?"

"One thing," Eddie said. "Just before the accident, I remembered something." He hesitated. "The Cronus night. I think I know who did it."

Preston perked up. "Really? Who?"

"A kid from the Island, raped a girl about a year or so before."

"And why do you think it's this person?" Preston asked, moving his hands together and tapping his fingertips.

116

"Because I saw him?"

"That night?"

"And," Eddie said, "maybe the night of the rape."

Preston was staring at him now. "You're making this connection now?"

"I know how it sounds?"

"How?" Preston asked.

"It sounds like I'm inventing it, I know..."

"Why would you do that?"

"I wouldn't."

"You said it..."

Eddie stopped talking and stared back. He should have seen this coming. "It came to me, I don't know, in a dream, or a drunken haze..." He stopped short. He wanted to take the words back as soon as they left his mouth. "I saw someone in the marsh that night. The same kid."

Preston relaxed. "A dream? You want me to believe the rapist and the murderer were the same person because you dreamt it?"

"It's not like I saw it in a dream, it got me thinking about it and when I stopped drinking, I had a better picture of things. I started to remember."

"How long had you stopped drinking when you got this *picture*?" His voice was a little less sincere.

"Two weeks," Eddie said, "and change."

"And are you still sober?"

He didn't answer. Preston was looking at him half out of concern and half out of aggravation. Eddie wished he'd never brought it up. Maybe he hadn't thought it through, what it would look like. "Fucked up, huh?" he said, searching for a way out.

"Ya, fucked up," Preston answered.

Eddie felt the blow.

"Are you all right?" Preston asked.

He felt trapped now. "Sure," Eddie said. "Right as rain."

Preston kept his eyes straight.

"What about these other two guys in the marsh?"

"We're all concerned," Preston said.

"Is Fisher still sniffing my ass hairs?" *A counter punch.*

The two men stared at each other, then Eddie worked his way out of the chair, and tucked the box under one arm. "I'd like to think you were all as concerned about finding who hit us that night?"

"Hit and run, Eddie," Preston said. "You know the odds, no witnesses, nothing but tire treads in a monsoon."

"If I was an active uniform, they'd still be looking."

"What does that mean?"

"Take it any way you want." He faced Preston. "And just for kicks," he said. "Did the kid who raped that girl ever turn up?"

"I'll look into it," Preston said. "But people disappear, Eddie, sometimes forever. Doesn't mean they killed anyone."

"No, it doesn't. Just a dream, right, Lieutenant." He turned to walk out of the office but stopped and looked back one more time. "About Fisher though. Don't fuck with me too much, Al," he said. "I've got nothing left to lose."

"Another time then," Preston said, but Eddie was already gone, and Preston knew the last word had been said.

Eddie threw the box in the back seat and drove away from the station. "Fuck him," he whispered to himself, stopping at a liquor store around the corner for a pint of vodka and a pack of cigarettes.

He took a few healthy hits off the bottle before beating a couple of lights on Broadway and crossing the circle onto the Marsh Road. By the time he reached Oak Island, more clouds had rolled in, and the sky was darkening.

He pulled across the street from a blue-sided house just off the road. The paint was peeling, and the porch sagged. *The Devil's lair.* He looked down the alleyway next to it to be sure and saw a car still on blocks in the backyard. Even though he was drunk that night, he could still see the uniforms standing on the porch with the old man, and the young girl with her father on the sidewalk a few houses down.

The lights were on upstairs and in the back. He hit the pint again and watched. Someone was home. After a few more minutes, he walked up the first few steps slowly. The porch creaked as he pulled a rusted metal storm door open and knocked on the wooden door behind it. No answer. He knocked again. This time he heard, "coming," from somewhere inside the house.

A few seconds later, after some fumbling with the locks, the door opened. A man stood there staring back, gray hair, glasses. "Ya," he said. "Can I help you?"

"Have you seen your son lately?" Eddie asked

"What are you talking about?" the man said.

"Your son, the rapist?"

"Who the fuck are you, you son of bitch," the man yelled. "Get off my porch."

Eddie backed up and the man asked again, "Who the fuck are you?"

"Police," he said.

"Show me a badge."

Eddie kept retreating to the end of the porch. The man came outside, put his hands on his hips. "What's your name?" he yelled, but Eddie was already hobbling across the street. When he got in his car and drove away, the man was still standing in the same place, like a statue, worn from the weather.

Chapter Forty

The night Eddie came out of his coma and was moved from intensive care, Joe Stang had pulled his car into the parking lot adjacent to the China Jade, just over the G.E. Bridge from Lynn. The business had shut down a little over a year ago for failure to pay back taxes, and now a group of Russians rented it. They stocked the bar, kept the lights on, had birthday parties, christenings, and met once a week to play cards.

He knocked on the worn wooden front door, looked up behind him at the neon martini glass hovering twenty feet above the building on a metal frame, no longer blinking like the night Michelle Letti drove away to her death in the marsh. He held the small canvas bag tightly under one arm and knocked again.

Finally, a tall man with a Red Sox hat pulled the door open. "Ya," he said.

"Jurek here?"

"Who are you?" the man asked with a thick Slavic accent.

"Tell him, Father Joe," Stang said.

The door closed, and he waited with an ear to it. He watched the traffic going over the bridge, two lanes, the tires moaning over the green iron grate. It made him think about when he was a new cop, driving the cruiser over that bridge, glad to be in uniform. Times were different then, less of the wise guy shit that soon followed, less of the drugs, right? Cops back then handled things, he thought to himself, *they were good, weren't they? Even he was a better man back in the day.*

The door whipped open again and Jurek, tall with a week-old beard and a black tee-shirt, motioned him in.

They stood in a mirrored hallway, the lights from the

barroom peeking in beyond. "Father Joe," Jurek said. "I like that."

Stang handed him the bag.

Jurek blessed himself, laughing. "You want to hear my confession, Padre?"

"I doubt it."

Jurek shook the bag a little and smiled. "Keep the sinners coming, Father."

Stang's face hardened. He stepped a little closer. "Let's not misunderstand each other. We aren't buddies."

"No," Jurek said. "Not until you need me." The smile was gone from his face too.

Stang knew what he was dealing with. The eyes staring back at him were dark and focused. The joking only a temporary way of being human.

"Until next time," Jurek told him.

Stang drove away from the parking lot, feeling like he always felt when he had these meetings, disturbed by the company he kept. There are always concessions, he thought. After all, the work wouldn't mean anything without the moral question; he was sure of that. He'd had his own losses, the cruel world of injustice had knocked hard on his door when he was a kid, and he knew others who were beaten, shot, raped, victims, who never had the pleasure of closure, never were vindicated by putting the scum who walked the earth behind bars, or better still, knowing they paid with their worthless lives.

He did what he did, and then he repented. Every week he knelt behind the thick red drapes of the confessional and told father Brice the veiled version of his actions.

"Bless me, Father, for I have sinned..."

"How have you sinned?"

"I am responsible for bad men getting what they deserve."

"Are you sorry?"

"Only for my part in it..."

"We're all imperfect. Ask for forgiveness."

"Thank you, Father."

"Do you think you've done the Lord's work?"

"I do."

"Then go forth and be saved. God will judge us all in the end. Ten Hail Marys and an Act of Contrition."

If it were only that easy, Stang thought, kneeling to pray at the altar afterwards. He knew first-hand the fine line between a martyr and a sinner.

Chapter Forty-One
The Beast

John Allen lived at the end of Lancaster Ave, by the beach road that ran along the rim of the Point of Pines. He lived with his mother, a born again Christian who read Bible passages out loud all day. His father was doing twenty in Walpole for attempted murder. John did his best to stay out of trouble, but his wanderings always seemed to lead him to the wrong people. Often, he owed money to guys you shouldn't owe money to, but most of them let him slide because they knew his old man. He was playing a Pac Man arcade machine his father had taken from a local barroom when Kyle Hardy showed up at his basement door. John looked him in the eye and knew something was different about him.

"Hey, Kyle. What's up, man. "

"Surprised to see me?"

"Fucking A. It's been, what, a year almost?"

"I thought maybe I could crash here for a few hours."

John led him into the basement apartment, one big room with small rectangle windows looking out to the street, a big television screen and a refrigerator against a blue cinder block wall.

"What's in the fridge?" Kyle asked.

"Go for it," *John told him. Kyle was already opening the door and grabbing a beer.*

"Where've you been anyway?" *John asked.*

"Florida," *he lied.*

"Doing what?"

"Working. Laying low."

"My mom knows about the rape. Everyone knows. If she finds you here, she'll call the cops."

Kyle stared at him, the hair hanging in his face, and John could smell him now, a strong body odor. He had a blank look, confused and, at the same time angry like John had said the wrong thing. "Ya, I know," he said and downed his beer.

He put the empty can down, stared back at John for a second, then made a gun sign with his thumb and forefinger, put it to his head, and pretended to squeeze the trigger. "Life sucks and then you die, right?"

"You want another one?" John asked.

Kyle popped the second beer in the doorway before leaving, raised it once like he was making a toast, then turned and walked to the street. John watched him moving toward the G.E. Bridge, the distant headlights crossing into Lynn. Kyle tilted his head back one more time, tossed the empty can against the front door of a house. A dog started barking.

At the end of street he turned left toward North Shore road and the train tracks that led to Oak Island.

Chapter Forty-Two

A month after the Grand Marquis flipped on top of Eddie and Gwen in the marsh, Roman pushed the long wooden gates of the junkyard together, ran a chain through the slats of rotting wood, and padlocked it. He walked further into the yard, past the trailer, the approaching dusk hanging over him. When the last phone call came, he'd come clean about that night, fessed up to Stang, told him he didn't know Devlin and his wheelchair date were near the car. "Fuck," he said to him. "I'm not stupid enough to kill a cop, even a looney one." He told him he was just paying him back for an old score, a bike he mangled. "An eye for an eye, right?" Roman laughed.

Stang didn't. "Burn the truck," he said. Roman protested, but Stang fired back. "Just do it now and lock the gates."

"And how do I make a living?"

"Consider yourself on vacation," Stang said.

Roman moved past the line of dented cars and pickup trucks that were left to rust and die. He was one of the only ones who ventured this far back in the yard, him and Eddie Devlin (to visit his ghost) and the occasional self-made mechanic looking to strip a clutch or a tie rod from one of the twisted metal skeletons. Otherwise, these cars sat alone like graveyard relics in a museum.

A black tow truck with a wide metal bumper was parked behind a stacked pile of burnt car bodies. The bumper's front plate had deep fresh grooves dug into the black paint. Roman started it and pulled it out onto the dirt road away from the other cars. At the rear of the truck, he opened a gas can, poured gas on the hood, and on the back of the bay. He took a rag from his back pocket, soaked it, removed the gas cap, and stuffed the rag in its place. Then he opened the passenger side door and put the can on the floor.

As he pulled a lighter from his pocket, something made him look away. When he did, he smiled. "Comrade. What gives?" he asked.

Three quick shots rang out, a neat cluster, all piercing Roman's forehead. He fell back against the truck seat and stood that way, half in and half out, and the lighter fell from his fingers onto the dirt.

Across the marsh, from the backside of Revere Beach Boulevard, a distant flame burned against the silhouette of the black dump hills, the marsh weeds, the train tracks running past Dizzy bridge. No one paid any attention to it driving up Route One. The yard was always burning something. It burned all night, the plume of smoke filling the junkyard sky until morning.

Chapter Forty-Three

The dog track was open early, celebrating something Eddie couldn't figure out. They were giving away scratch tickets and coupons that were good for hot dogs at the concession stand— anything to get them in, make them study the program like college students cramming for a final.

Eddie walked past the infield doors and into the clubhouse bar. He unzipped his leather jacket, glanced behind him at the crowd still hustling in for the double. Lately, he felt like people were following him.

Dana was by himself, standing at the dark wood bar. Eddie limped over, trying to use the cane less, the little reminders of muscle memory running up and down his body, the drugs and the booze keeping the worst of them at bay.

When he got close, Dana held the sheet up with a few of the entries circled. "You want winners?"

"Not those, you mean?" Eddie asked, leaning into the bar.

"Your loss."

"You're looking like you could run a marathon," Dana said.

"Have another donut."

"No shit. Moving pretty good for a cripple."

Eddie stared back, a slight smile. "I'm moving. Better than not, right?"

"Sometimes," Dana said, looking into the program. "Depends on how many races you hit. The car run all right?"

"Ya."

"Keep it as long as you want or until some big Canuck comes looking for it."

Eddie looked over his shoulder then back to Dana. "You know that weasel, who asked about me at the diner?"

"Fisher," Dana answered, circling another winner.

"Have you seen him here? Other than tonight, I mean."

Dana perked up. "He's here?" he asked.

Eddie looked over the crowd sitting in the room, mostly men gathered at tables full of empties, smoke curling to the corners of the ceiling. "Outside I think, by the infield."

"Maybe he likes the dogs."

"Maybe," Eddie said. "Going up?"

"What do you want?"

"Pick one. Twenty on the nose." He handed Dana two tens.

Beyond the glass to the infield, the betters hustled to the fence by the track like their yelling was going to make the dogs go faster. Eddie scanned the crowd feeling like he was on some close circuit television, maybe a telescope or God on a satellite working for the RPD.

Dana slapped the ticket down. "Number five, Golden Boy."

"Thanks, chief. I'll cut you in."

The dogs rounded the first turn, the cheers of the faithful on the rail, the clubhouse crowd erupting. The five ran third the whole race, finished with a show and paid two dollars and fifty cents.

"Should have bet him across the board," Eddie said.

"Should have," Dana said and walked off toward the window, Eddie knew, to cash a ticket. Just beyond him on the other side of the glass doors, he saw Ron Fisher making his way to the exit, a tan Barracuda jacket and a baseball cap. He never looked Eddie's way, just walked straight and joined the crowd exiting down the ramp and out of sight.

Eddie stayed two more races, drew a photo in the last one, but in the end, he lost them both. After a beer in the parking lot, he drove up the Legion Highway to Broadway. The streets were deserted this time of night; the stores all closed, just the lights from the barrooms every other block, and a few kids hanging on the corner. He rode by two cruisers in a late-night donut shop parking lot, laughed a little to himself. "I probably know the bums," he said. He could go in if he wanted to, have a cup and a chat. They were all brothers, right? They could talk about the state of the city or the way things used to be as if the passage of time always made things better.

He drove three miles to the Marsh Road, thinking about how he had accused Preston of ignoring the accident, but that was mostly frustration. Eddie was tired of not knowing things, and he couldn't keep waiting for the news he knew was never going to come.

When he pulled in front of the gates to the junkyard, he noticed the padlock and the heavy chain pulled through the wooden slats. He opened the trunk, looked unsuccessfully for a flashlight, then reached in the driver-side window and put the headlights on. They cast bright beams all the way to Roman's trailer. The windows were dark, and there were no bikes parked in front of it.

As he stepped into the mud and weeds around one side of the gate, he saw a cardboard sign on the ground that read 'closed' in faded black marker.

He put a foot on the first step and looked back at the headlights shining toward him. Suddenly he got dizzy; *the headlights were moving, coming closer, the rain hitting him in the face, his hand trying to pull Gwen away.* A bat flew out into the light, from the half-open trailer door. Eddie ducked as it came at him, then stood and watched the bat disappear into the night sky. He scanned the wasteland around him. The yard was deathly quiet, just the crickets, and the occasional car driving by out front.

When he pushed the trailer door open with his cane, a sliver of light shone through a small window at the top of the wall. It smelled like the rest of the junkyard, moldy and decaying. He could make out the top of a desk and a lamp without a shade behind a pile of papers. After he fumbled for the lamp switch and managed to turn it on, a dim glow reflected off the walls.

The trailer was pretty much the same since Eddie had set foot in it the last time. Two years ago, he stood in front of the same desk questioning Roman about a possible runaway. "I know how helpful you can be to wandering teens," he said.

"I'm a generous guy," Roman answered.

Eddie held up a picture, a sixteen-year-old blonde girl.

"I'd remember her, Detective."

"There's a reward," Eddie told him. "The father's rich."

That was a lie. The girl's father worked in the baggage claim at the airport, but Eddie had figured it might keep Roman's hands off her if she did show up.

He pulled a drawer open and felt around inside, more papers, a pack of cigarettes, some plastic utensils, and a flashlight. He clicked it on and let it shine across the desk, then looked closer at the pile of papers. They were mostly ledgers for tows, Revere, Lynn, Swampscott. Some were billed to the police, all six months or later. In the top drawer, he pulled out a few utility bills for an apartment in Revere, an overdue mechanic's bill (probably somebody Roman was screwing), and more tow slips. He sifted through old pin-up calendars and receipts from a hardware store on Shirley Ave, and a bank statement showing a checking account with five hundred dollars and change.

In another drawer, he found a blue glass bong, a razor package, and a small mirror with white residue around the edges. The last drawer was empty except for a box of rubbers unopened in a blue Trojan box.

Some flies flew past him as he moved near some indecipherable garbage in the sink. The empty cabinet doors were open, and three plastic bags of trash sat in the middle of the floor. Eddie kicked one, heard the rumblings of cans.

At the back of the trailer, he slid a plastic divider open and flicked the light switch on the wall, revealing a stained mattress against the fake wood paneling. The mattress was partially covered with a yellow sheet. Empty beer bottles stood on the small window ledge over a poster of Elvis Presley. "The sick fuck thinks it's his jungle room," Eddie whispered.

He went back to the desk and combed through the tow slips again. One of them jumped out at him— a tow from the Marsh Road a few months ago. Just said RPD, no name.

Something stirred outside, moving through the junk. *Rats.* He gathered the slips and stuffed them into his back pocket.

When he walked back into the yard, the moon shone from behind the clouds like a stage spotlight. He could see for a hundred yards in front of him under it, but it didn't last long. The clouds moved back quickly, and he was left with the narrow beam of the flashlight to guide him.

The route to the back of the yard was familiar, winding its way through scattered piles of junk, tires, hubcaps, tailpipes, and mufflers. Even with the light moving from side to side, he tapped his cane as a warning to whatever was out there.

Once he realized he was out of range of his headlights, the path ahead seemed longer and darker than he'd remembered.

After a few minutes, he approached the line of car bodies he'd come to know, and moved the light down the end of the row to Michelle Letti's white Buick, still parked where he'd told Roman to leave it. The other cars all had their own horror stories, too.

A burnt tow truck was pulled out in front of the line. He moved around it carefully, back to front, the charred truck bed, the tires melted on all fours, the windows shattered. It was like the truck had become part of the earth, slowly sucked into the sludge below it. A soft but shrill sound made him shiver. He reached for the scorched door, opened it slowly, and it slipped a few inches from the hinges, heavy in his hand, the metal creaking.

The first thing he saw on top of the exposed seat cushion springs, next to the deformed and melted steering wheel and dashboard, was a tarnished silver belt buckle, then the black bone, connected to what might have been a pile of rotted, burnt, and decayed flesh. He heard the noise again and saw a rat sitting on its hind legs at the head of the body, chewing.

When he moved the flashlight to the side, there were a dozen of them scurrying away from the light, some jumping out the shattered windows across from him, some running in his direction, brushing by his legs, a few others staying put, chewing what remained of the decomposed person on the seat.

Chapter Forty-Four

Any midnight on the weekend and the beach could still be cooking, headlights from one end to the other, muffled heavy metal from tinted windows, a Harley or two weaving in and out the traffic, the Boston skyline looming in the distance. The beach people doing beach things.

Dennis Morris spent his life here, watching it all go by, sometimes at work, sometimes looking out the window of Micky's barroom. They were his people, the ones who worked it and played on it. The beach brought them all together, he figured, a long line of accumulated misery. "If he's buying, I'm flying. Put it on ice, Marie. I'll get to it, sure as shit," he often said.

Marie worked the tap at Mickey's, the little stone building halfway down the boulevard from the Lynn line, two empty lots on either side. Dennis drank here every night after frying clams all day. He was always waxing philosophical like this, spouting off to Marie, "If you spent the day sifting buckets of cornmeal and white flour, breading shellfish with your fingers, you'd throw a few back wouldn't you?" Marie and the small crowd of locals would cheer and sling another round of suds like they were warriors in some medieval mead hall.

In other years he'd had conversations from various payphones in the dark hallways of different bar rooms. *Hey, I'll be home soon, just stopped in for a couple.* And always back at the bar ordering two more.

The girlfriends were another lifetime ago. Now Dennis was alone, a two-room flat on the end of the strip. The stand where he worked and Mickey's were all he had. He was on a string between them. His last relationship had ended when he'd gotten drunk one night, passed out on the floor of his apartment, and woke up to the police pounding on his door. Ellen Kelly, his former girlfriend of two years, had pulled a domestic abuse warrant on him. She claimed he came home and wanted sex, and when she had said no, he hit her, then tried to strangle her on the bed. She had marks on her throat and a slight bruise below her eye. True, he hadn't ever done it before, hadn't ever hit anyone for that matter, but it wasn't the first time he blacked out from drinking too much. Even though he knew he didn't do it, he had no way to defend it. They hadn't even gone out in months, but she had come by that night and asked to crash on his couch.

On the day she filed against him, she came by again after he posted bail and told him she'd drop the charges for a thousand bucks, which he borrowed to make it go away.

He figured she had it done or did it to herself. He knew why too. For the shit. She had taken to the needle full time, just before they split up for good.

So, he went off to live with the blackout hanging over him until she knocked on his door six months later and wanted more money. She threatened to file again. He told her no, and she left his apartment yelling, "you'll see."

It never happened, though. Ellen wound up dead in an alley by the North Gate shopping plaza, a couple of miles from the beach. She'd been hit in the head and dumped there. Eddie Devlin had been one of the cops on the case and had come to Dennis's apartment to bring him in for questioning.

Eventually Dennis was cleared of any connection to the murder (though it remained unsolved). Ellen's sister, Janice, a dancer at the Surf Club, and a friend of the department took it upon herself to drag him through the newspapers, accusing him of her sister's murder. She wouldn't let it go, not even a year later when they discovered Ellen owed drug money to a gang on the Ave. Still, Janice spread the rumor every chance she got. Most people thought it got too crazy, but she had her supporters, among them, the cops with the cold cases in the basement of the RPD.

Dennis got paranoid after that. Every stranger's question

felt like an accusation. He did his best to stay in the shadows, but it felt like a matter of time before something fell hard on him.

One night, after tying one on, he shuffled his way up Revere Street and stopped to piss in the alley by the cigar store across from St. Theresa's. He relieved himself and was smiling at the sensation when he heard two voices on the sidewalk. The name 'Devlin' made his ears perk up. The conversation was low at first, but as he focused, he could hear it better. *Devlin, the Cronus shit.*

The first voice said, "Where do we see this going? I want this over with."

Then the other, "It will be soon."

"I don't know what that means."

"It means..." The voice cut off, then finished, "soon."

"I'm not so sure."

"Do you remember why this got started?"

"I'm not fucking stupid."

"Then you'll know why we have no choice. We're all in this together."

"And him?"

"We both agreed there'd be damage. You signed on knowing that."

There was a beat, then they started again. Dennis stood still and listened to the two men finish their conversation.

When everything was quiet, except the slight traffic on North Shore Road, he stepped out onto the sidewalk. Joe Stang let himself in the front door of the church across the street. Dennis started to walk, glanced back once more over his shoulder, and saw Ron Fisher standing a few yards away smoking a cigar. They stared at each other for a second, and Dennis recognized him as a former cop. *Does he know who I am? Fuck, they all know.* He heard the church door close, turned and walked quickly up the street.

Chapter Forty-Five

Eddie got into a routine after seeing what he was sure was Roman's charred body in the junkyard that night. He went from the racetrack to the corner stool at Dana's, maybe a side trip to the beach for pizza or fried clams. The sameness of things might have kept him from going nuts. He won money some nights and lost some others, but he always ended up comfortably numb by closing time at his favorite armrest. Three times in the last week he'd taken the cot instead of driving home or getting a cab. One night he passed out face first on the bar before closing. He apologized the next morning, but Dana just blew it off. "Twenty years in the bar business and that's going to get me? Some big mick taking a nap," Dana said. "The guy on the next stool just kept talking to you." Even though Eddie laughed a little at that, he felt a pang of guilt. He used to be able to hold his tea. At one time, he took pride in that.

He called Preston about the body. Preston asked Eddie to come into the office again. What started out as two cops talking ended up with Preston lecturing him.

"Stop playing detective on private property," Preston said. "I don't care what you find."

"Eddie told him to fuck off, and Preston finally lost his temper, called him a drunk, and suggested he get some serious help soon, before it was too late.

"And I got a call about a cop harassing a guy," Preston said. "Ray Hardy. Ring a bell?"

"Nope."

"Kyle Hardy's father. The kid who raped that girl in the marsh."

"Oh ya, Hardy," Eddie said.

"He gave me a description. I told him I'd look into it."

"Did you?"

"I am now," Preston said. "This is your last warning, Eddie, cop or no cop. If you ever want to move on with your life, stop fucking drinking."

When Eddie got to the track that night, he took it easy, only four races and three beers. He got back to his apartment about ten. The lights from the G.E. Bridge were blinking in the distance. He parked the Mustang in the driveway and stepped out slowly. When he straightened up and started to walk, something in the street caught his eye.

About halfway up the street, parked on the opposite side, was a dark-colored four-door sedan, a few years old, a used department issue. Eddie looked in that direction a couple more seconds, then walked up the stairs and let himself in.

Once inside, he hustled best he could through the back door and onto a tiny porch landing. He hurried down the four steps to the concrete backyard then around the side of the house by way of a skinny alley, where he kept two plastic trash barrels and a broken-down lawnmower.

He stepped through the uncut hedges into the neighbor's yard, hit his leg against a rusted metal fence post and let out a muffled, "fuck." The limp got worse for a few steps as he moved onto the front lawn of the third house down from him. He was across from the sedan now. The motor was running, and he knew he only had a few seconds.

After circling back behind the car, he hunched as best as he could by the rear bumper and then moved along the side to the back seat window. He held the cane in one hand, tossed it on the front hood, and grabbed the driver's side door handle and whipped it open. The move made every muscle in his body ache, but he was working on adrenaline. He grabbed Ron by the collar, yanked with all his strength, and fell to the ground on top of him. He was careful to note the hands before anything else, in case Ron reached for his gun. When he saw them empty, he landed one hard punch to the nose and scooted his knees up to his shoulders and held him down.

136

The pain in his legs and back was frightening now, shooting hot wires to every fiber of his body, but he held his ground and yelled, "You motherfucker."

He raised his hand to punch one more time, but Ron deflected it, and the two rolled over each other into the street. Eddie managed to grab a headlock, but Ron repeatedly punched his stomach until he let go, and he rolled Eddie one more time, face-first into the street, and twisted his arm behind his back.

Eddie screamed into the night, from anger, from pain, "Motherfucker."

Ron was bleeding from the nose. He leaned into Eddie's ear. "Listen you piece of shit. I'd just as soon as pop one in your brain. Don't give me a fucking reason."

A few houses around them had turned on the porch lights. A dog was barking somewhere.

"I'm going to let you up," Ron said, "before a uniform shows up and has to haul your sorry ass in."

He let the arm go.

Eddie struggled to his knees and sat back on his legs; his head bent. Ron stood over him, backed up a few feet, then grabbed the cane off the hood. He put it on the ground in front of Eddie, who used it to get to his feet, straightened up, and walked toward the gray-stucco house.

Ron stared at him moving under the street light as he wiped the blood from his nose on his sleeve. He waited for something else, a look, a parting threat, but Eddie never turned around. He kept limping along the sidewalk, the darkness surrounding him, until he disappeared into the house.

Chapter Forty-Six

Eddie was fighting for breath by the time he made it to the couch. His chest was tight, and the throbbing in his body played a steady beat in his ears. He wasn't sure what was worse, the anger or the pain coursing through him. He sat, felt the sting on his back from the skin that scraped off in the street. His muscles were tightening up and down his arms, and a few times he was sure he was going to pass out.

After a few minutes, he made his way to the kitchen, where he took a bottle from the cabinet and poured himself a straight one in a water glass. By the time he filled it a third time, and swallowed a Percocet, he was back on the couch smoking a cigarette and feeling like his old broken self again.

He closed his eyes, let the numbing take hold, and walked to the window in the living room. Fisher and his car were gone, and once again, the neighborhood was under the curtain of civility. A cruiser moved slowly past the dark houses, just headlights, probably responding to an earlier call about a disturbance in the street.

When Eddie sat back down, his eyes landed on the shoebox of Gwen's things he'd taken home from the station. He reached over and put it in his lap, pulled the brown cover off, and instantly smelled something sweet. He rummaged through, found a package of mints in a plastic bag tied with a red ribbon. The card attached to it said, *To Eddie, Merry Christmas.* "She forgot," he said to himself, smiling. "Fucking space shot."

His fingers searched the box again: a Robert Parker novel, probably had the overdue library tag in the back with his name on it, and two photographs. One was of Gwen and him sitting on the sea wall eating clams. Eddie remembered the day. A little guy who walked the boulevard and always wore a quilted vest had taken it with a Polaroid camera. He smiled after shaking it and waiting for it to develop.

Gwen gave him ten dollars for it.

Eddie looked at the photo now, the beach sky a streak of blue, a few seagulls hovering over their shoulder. *I was thinner then,* he thought, and he realized Gwen was sitting with her wheelchair out of the shot. There was something uncomfortably normal about it.

The other photo was Eddie alone outside the Brattle theater, a Cagney double-feature advertised behind him on the sidewalk marquee. He was wearing a leather jacket and smoking a cigarette, trying to look like a real gangster himself.

He reached in one more time and lifted a white mug with his name on it, then underneath it in the bottom of the box, a newspaper clipping from the day. *"Cronus in the Marsh?"* The front page was folded once like a subway read and again into a square. *Why would she?* and in that instant, a sadness fell over him like a blanket.

He cried one soft sob looking into the box, wanting to wish for something but not being sure what. And then from deep inside, the tears came quickly, bursting with all the sadness in his life, all the sadness in anyone's life, his father and his mother watching their son self-destruct, all the parents who had to call a cop, all the dummies who got mixed up with the wrong scum, all the Michelle Lettis and the Gwens, all of them crashing down onto his shoulders, and he fell to the floor on his knees, the newspaper in one hand, the photo on the beach in the other, and rolled onto his side like a baby.

Chapter Forty-Seven

Dana came by the next morning after Eddie called him. He sat on the couch, took the cup of coffee Eddie carried from the kitchen. "I'll risk it," he said.

"It's fresh," Eddie insisted and sat down next to Dana, squinting from the new soreness.

"You all right?" Dana asked.

"Beating on a cripple. Even for him, a new low."

The two men sampled the coffee in silence.

"Not bad," Dana said, putting the cup down on the corner of the couch. "Your buddy in the junkyard finally went fishing."

"I'm not crying," Eddie said. "But that was no accident."

"There must have been a line to pop that prick."

"Probably," Eddie said. "And Preston taking a burn I found the body, is that fucked up?"

Dana listened, sipped more coffee.

"I'm just trying to figure out who wanted to kill me... right? It seemed to me like a good place to start," Eddie said. "Is that so fucking weird?"

"What's weird," Dana said, "is usually scum like that lives forever." He lit a cigarette, threw the pack to Eddie. "Do you remember Vinny, what the fuck was his last name? Nestor, I think, always fed the pigeons on the beach by the first circle."

"Sure, when I was a kid. Crazy Vinny?"

"He broke legs his whole life, did a short bid in Concord for crushing some kid's skull."

"What about him?"

"He lived to be about ninety. Died in Miami on the beach, sucking rum drinks."

"So."

"So that's my point. The worst of them live forever."

"Now, you're a philosopher."

"Just an observer," Dana said and drained his cup. "But since I'm playing it. Dig this. You're never going to get them all. Sometimes the bad guys win."

Eddie sat there, silent for a moment. He knew what Dana was getting at.

"As I see it you've got two choices," Dana said, "stop looking for ghosts and get on with your life."

"Or?"

"Or don't."

Eddie took a breath. "And Preston sending his best boy to tail me?" he asked, "when does he get on with his?"

"He'll get tired and it'll be like it never happened."

"That's the problem, isn't it?" Eddie asked. "Everything disappears. But I never know why, or who or where?"

Dana let the conversation hang there for a second. "What are you doing tonight?" he asked.

"Let me think," Eddie said. "What did I do last night?"

Dana shifted in his seat, pulled two tickets from his pocket. "Celtics, Knicks, two rows up."

Eddie stared at the tickets. "It has been a while."

"The preacher on the street told me he found them, traded them for two drinks."

"God must be a fan, too," Eddie said.

"No," Dana told him. "The preacher moonlights as a pickpocket."

The Green Line subway ran overhead along Causeway Street, in front of The Boston Garden, the connected green cars turning the corner and squeaking to a stop above North Station. They walked down the stairs, Eddie limping over each step, Dana moving just as slow on purpose. They walked two blocks past the bars and the pizza places, and one Italian restaurant parking cars in the lot. They crossed the street by Sullivan's Tap. A man and his girlfriend were out front arguing, a couple of guys on the next corner were hawking tickets, a few cops rode by on horseback.

The Garden doors were open, and they walked up the winding ramp, like a sand castle slide that led to the ticket gate. Once inside, Dana pointed to their section. "I'll get us a beer," he said. "Go sit."

It seemed brighter than Eddie remembered, the familiar wood-green seats of the balcony above him, the banners, fifteen of them hanging from the rafters, the organ music playing from the far corner. The stands were buzzing already as he made his way to the second row, sat closest to the aisle, and watched the Celtics warming up, Bird, Maxwell, Chief, D.J. The two-line drill was his favorite—the smooth precision.

Dana sat with the two beers, handed him one, pulled a pretzel from his pocket, and broke it in half. "Celtics minus twelve," he said.

"A suckers bet," Eddie said. "Bernard could have fifty."

"That's it though."

They looked toward the Knick's end. Bernard King did a three-sixty dunk in the layup line and the crowd reacted.

The Celtics went up by thirteen at the half. King had twenty, Bird, a dozen. Dana went to fetch a few more beers. As Eddie watched the teams coming out for second half warm-ups, he remembered a night he played on this floor, a state championship game against Don Bosco High school. He'd gone to the line with thirteen seconds left, up one. He made both and they won by a point. If he could have frozen time there, the crowd cheering, his father's voice above them all, the ball falling through the net, everything in his mind quiet, confident, the road ahead of him filled with promise, he would have.

Dana passed a beer over as the second half started with a flurry by the Knicks, cutting the lead to three. By the fourth quarter, the Celts pushed it back to ten on three straight buckets by Maxwell and a dunk by Chief. King ended up with thirty-nine. The Celtics won by eleven.

On the subway ride home, Eddie asked Dana, "How much

did that cost you? I know you never bet against the good guys."

"Small change," Dana said.

Small change to Eddie and small change to Dana were two different brands of silver.

When they got back, Dana let the bartender go home. It was just him and Eddie after he locked the door. They each had a drink and a smoke going.

"That preacher friend of yours has a link to some fine seats," Eddie said. "Fucker's got it made."

"I'm not sure about that."

"He's crazy, right, but everyone thinks he's crazy, so no one is surprised. He walks up and down the street, waving his cross, yelling the name of the Lord. Everyone is okay with it."

"I don't see where this is going."

"If people expect you to be nuts, you just carry on. Doing what you're good at."

"You're drunk," Dana said. He was right, he was drunk.

"I'm serious. People think I'm nuts, but I'm not expected to be, so they send guys to tail me, to prove I'm nuts, or dangerous, or whatever the fuck they're trying to prove. The preacher gets to roll along crazy as a loon. Just another day at the office."

Dana wiped the bar, crushed a cigarette in the ashtray.

"You know, I told Preston I thought I knew who killed the Letti girl that night," Eddie said.

"Do you know?"

"Good question."

"What did he say?"

"It's what he didn't say." Eddie took a big breath. "If you were me..."

"I'd pray more," Dana interrupted.

"Really? What would you do?"

"I don't know, Eddie." He tossed the rag behind him. "I guess I'd sleep on it. But I wouldn't be in a hurry to go chasing things in the dark, not anymore. It ain't getting you anywhere. I'd be sure before I did the next thing."

Eddie put the empty beer on the bar. "Thanks for the game."

"You want a cab?"

"No. I'm fucking crazy, right? I'll be all right," he yelled, walking out into the night. As the door shut behind him, he thought to himself, *don't you worry. I'll be sure.*

Dana knew what he said to Eddie was a lie. If his friend had gotten killed, he'd never stop looking for answers, no matter how remote or insignificant the clues. He knew he'd react to every possibility, even the stupid ones, driven by senseless gut feelings. And, he knew it would haunt him, just like it was haunting Eddie. Lying to him about it, was the only way he knew how to be a friend.

Chapter Forty-Eight

Two weeks later, it snowed, not much, just a dusting, but enough to muck things up for the morning commute, get people flocking to the hardware stores for shovels and rock salt. It hadn't snowed before Thanksgiving in a few years, and the trees that weren't done shedding had heavy leaves covered in white frost. Even the treeless beach had a sheen of white powder on the sand.

Eddie parked the red Mustang near the circle at the Beachmont end, three miles from the Lynn line, stepped slowly out of the car, and left the cane on the seat. He wore a pair of old white canvas high cuts, sweat pants, and a hooded sweatshirt. He put two hands on the small of his back, bent slightly forward and backward, and instantly got light-headed. "Fuck," he groaned, looking at the gray-blue ocean, a few white caps gathering.

The past few weeks had allowed for a little more range of motion each day. Even the pain was better than it had been, almost bearable, not having to pop Percs all day to stand up.

He figured he'd walk the boulevard as far as Revere Street and back, two miles round trip. It was a start.

When he got to the first bathhouse, he saw a group of old guys sitting in a circle. They belonged to a club that sunbathed year-round and swam in the ocean on New Year's Day. The early winter breeze was blowing against their aluminum reflectors. Eddie knew a few of them. He kept his head down and walked past, ignored the same old conversation they were having, how great it was when the amusements ran for six months a year and the sailors danced with their dates under the lights on the pier. Eddie wanted to tell them living in the past will kill ya.

He was halfway to Revere Street when the cruiser pulled up behind him. A uniform was driving. Eddie turned and saw Preston getting out of the passenger side, a black topcoat over his suit.

"Training for another fight," he said and smiled.

"Fuck him," Eddie said. "He had it coming."

"Can we talk?"

"Are you taking me in?"

"No," Preston said, and waved the cruiser off. "Can I walk with you?"

"It's a free beach, for now anyway." He looked at the strip of new cement condos on Ocean Ave running parallel to the boulevard. "Though if they have their way..."

The two men walked close to the sea wall. Preston buttoned the neck of his coat.

"Did you really send the car home?" Eddie asked. "Or is he circling, making sure I don't drag you off into the marsh?"

"I don't think I'd go quietly."

"No, I don't suppose you would."

Preston was working it around in his head, the right way to say what he was about to say. Everything with him was a delicate balance between being a boss and being a human being. "I called him off, Eddie."

"Because."

"Because it's not the right thing to do anymore."

"But it had been?"

"Nothing you wouldn't have done if you were in my shoes."

"Maybe," Eddie said, looking across the street at two bearded guys holding brown bags in the alley between barrooms.

"Fisher does us a service, a service you'd agree with if it weren't you. He lets us stay involved in our own way, be discreet with ex-cops."

"Like the good old boys' club?" Eddie asked, looking Preston in the eyes, not expecting an answer. "Wait," he said. "Is this an apology?"

Preston held his hand out. "You know how it is, Eddie."

They shook. "Besides," he said, "you might want the job someday."

Eddie answered with a look that said *I don't think so.*

Preston reached into his coat, pulled out a photo of Kyle Hardy, standing in the yard with a fishing pole, the long hair hanging in his face. "I checked this from the file."

Eddie stared at it.

"This the kid you saw the night of the rape?"

"Maybe," Eddie said. "I told you I was drunk."

"What's your hunch?"

"My hunches haven't worked out so well lately, Lieutenant."

"He's still a missing person. No trace." Preston let it hang there.

"I guess some ghosts are real," Eddie said. The cruiser pulled up behind them. "Your ride's here."

"We'll keep the file open," Preston said, waved the photo, and turned and got in the passenger side. And that was that, just one more look between them.

When the cruiser pulled away, Eddie was almost to Revere Street, a little short of the intended goal. "Fuck it," he whispered and did an about-face and started back to the car.

Chapter Forty-Nine
The Beast

Kyle walked on the dark edges of the sidewalk, past the one convenient store in Oak Island, and kept to the shadows like a bat. He didn't care about the rain, wasn't even sure that rain was something that mattered to him anymore.

The streets felt different to him. Fucking shit hole, he thought, and wandered unconsciously through the backyards that bumped up to the marsh. When he got near his house, the familiar blue clapboards, the crooked porch, he saw the light in the living room window and heard the voices inside. He knew it was his father and a neighbor from down the street. They were laughing at something on the television.

He sat beneath the window on a porch step and listened to the steady beat of the rain off the gutters. Then his father laughed again, the way he used to when Kyle was a kid, when he'd throw bits of bread to the seagulls and stand in the middle of a circle of them, pretending they were attacking, no, no, no! Back when his mother was around.

For a split second he imagined sitting there with his father and his friend, telling raunchy jokes, drinking beer, but he knew it wasn't like that. The laugh bothered him, and he thought about the time his father beat him for stealing his booze, wrapped a belt around his knuckles and punched his cheeks until he spit blood.

He reached for carpet knife in the leather holster and ran his thumb over the blade. He pressed it into his skin until a warm sticky ooze covered his thumb. He stared again at the flicker of a television set bouncing off the walls, watched it dance to the rhythm of the rain, the wind, the tapping on the roof. He wasn't sure if he should go in or just wait for him outside, so he walked into the backyard, then deeper into the marsh where he could hide.

Then he heard it, not far away on the Marsh Road, the pop like a gunshot, then the tires crunching over the gravel shoulder. He walked towards it, the sound of the car door slamming, a girl's voice yelling "piece of shit tire." And the words took him like a siren, calling him home after a long time at sea.

Chapter Fifty

Eddie could feel the pain up the back of his legs when he stepped out of the car. He knew those first steps were going to be the worst, and it made him want to curl up into the blanket of painkillers. Instead, he sat on the couch, cracked a cold can of beer and lit a cigarette. The reward. He looked at the box Preston had given him at the station, turned on its side, and some of the contents spilled onto the floor, the white mug, the photos. He scooped everything back inside and put the box on his lap. His fingers roamed through the contents again, not looking, just feeling his way along. He picked up the Robert Parker novel and flipped the pages like watching one of those paper book movies from the carnival. Then he turned the book over, read the back cover. A tight Parker plot, internal corruption, a good cop gone wrong, and some former thug to set it straight. He opened it back to front and looked at the library card stuck in the plastic jacket, his name the last hand-written entry. A smile came to him slowly, and he remembered having taken the book out and Gwen's reaction when he showed up with it one day. "You don't get enough cop shit on the job?" she asked him.

"When you're right, you're right," he said and tossed the book onto her kitchen counter where it stayed until it got filed into the box after she died.

He tucked his fingers inside the plastic sleeve and tore down the seam, disconnecting one side of the sleeve from the page. "I don't want the library police after me," he whispered to himself. With a swift tug, he ripped the rest of it away, leaving a torn scar on the inside back cover. A piece of paper fell out from behind the plastic and landed on the floor. He picked it up. It was folded twice into a square. When he opened it, something in his gut instantly turned, and he felt his face get flush.

He looked closely along the left-hand margin and read quietly aloud the words on the page as if saying them might make them disappear. Written in Gwen's familiar scrawl was a list of names, *Tommy Mac, Gary Pitlor, Steve Salvi, Nick Cory, Pudge Bankia*— all of them names Eddie had heard of during police work, all of them with a black line running through them. The two other names at the bottom of the list were clean, with no lines crossing them out. One of them, *Dennis Morris,* Eddie remembered, was a former suspect in a murder case. The last name, though, was the one that hit him right between the eyes, *Kyle Hardy*.

Chapter Fifty-One

Hallelujah. Joe Stang stared at the image of Jesus on one knee, the way the cross held him to the ground, the weight he was bearing, the responsibility. He genuflected and moved to the next station.

Hallelujah. Christ betrayed. He felt the heat working through the pipes, the cold leaving for the rafters, just in time for five o'clock Mass. He knelt on one knee again.

Hallelujah. He stared at Christ on the cross. He knew every great deed had a sacrifice somewhere along the line. He'd worked this out in his mind enough to be sure. The world was a better place because of his deeds. He knew he was doing the Lord's work; he knew that night listening to the women tell their stories; they had been brutalized, victimized, and forgotten. He'd been a victim, Ron Fisher, too. They'd all paid the price. What could people do when the law let them down, when no more angels came to fight for them? Michael the Archangel was a warrior. Joe Stang was only carrying on the Christian tradition, carrying the ugly truth on a righteous banner, fighting for those who'd given up hope.

Hallelujah.

When he was done, he checked the thermostat, put his hand on the radiator behind the confessionals. Soon they would file in and take their place among the forgiven, and he would walk the aisle stretching the woven straw basket to each parishioner, waiting for the believers' gifts, knowing a portion of them would be working towards redemption. And he knew that he was righteous and that the Lord hired the sinners to do the work the saints couldn't do.

Chapter Fifty-Two

Gwen always filled the seats when she spoke, a library somewhere, a conference room, or this night, a church basement. Like other nights, she sat alone in her wheelchair with rows of women in front of her and two uniformed police standing by the door in the back. She greeted the crowd with immediate candor, telling them the way she felt after her attack, how she wanted revenge, specifically, and finally how she managed to move beyond it, even though she would never forget it.

Several women in the hall were crying at the end of the half-hour talk, which by this time in her career was polished, poignant, and empowering. She ended as always with, "if I can do it, this chair reminding me every day of the abuse, then you can do it. They've already taken a piece of your life. Don't let them take the rest of it."

She opened the floor to questions of which there were many. Procedural matters were referred to the police on-site, the more emotional ones she handled deftly.

Dennis Morris had walked into the hall during the middle of the talk. He sat on the aisle about halfway to the front, watching Gwen and the people in the room around him. After a few questions, he stood and blurted out. "What do you do when you've been falsely accused of abuse?" He was drunk. His words slurred.

Gwen handled it. "There are procedures. The law is here for everyone." The consensus in the room was when men like him invaded the meeting, they had personal legal agendas, and their outbursts were designed to make them look innocent for an upcoming defense. Most of this crowd tended not to believe claims like his and most of the time they were right. The two cops, who had moved up front to take questions, straightened up for action. "I don't mean with the cops," he said. "I mean with yourself."

"No one in this room wants to convict innocent people. Were you convicted of something?" Gwen asked, her voice a bit less patient with each answer.

Dennis swayed slightly and said, "I may as well have been," and walked from the room.

The hall remained silent for a few seconds after he left, then new questions popped up as if he were never there at all.

As Always, Gwen stayed and spoke to women individually for over an hour. As the hall cleared, Joe Stang came forward and took away the microphone stand, then wound the orange extension cord in a circle over his arm. When Gwen finished talking to one young girl, Stang started putting the chairs onto a four-wheeled dolly nearby.

Within minutes, they were the only two left in the church hall.

"Fancy seeing him here," Stang said with half a smile, stacking chairs.

"It's like he knows," Gwen said and wheeled past him and out the door.

Chapter Fifty-Three

The game had changed.

If what Eddie thought was true, that Gwen was somehow connected to the names on that list (and not just keeping a scorecard) then he needed to do what they paid him to do for twenty years. He didn't have many people he could count on to help. There was Dana, and then there was nobody.

He grabbed another cold beer from the ice behind the bar. The place was mostly empty, a few Vietnamese guys playing cards in a booth, and one guy nodding off on the other side of the room. Dana picked up the paper with the names on it. "Where are these guys? Dead? MIA?" he asked.

Each one had been accused of abuse but never convicted. That much Eddie knew. That's what kept them together in a tidy little cluster. Tommy Mac had been close to jail for years before he disappeared. Eddie was sure he'd been arrested for battery a few times, once he knew on a stripper he was dating. Pitlor was a notorious drug dealer with enough dirt to bury him three times over. Salvi was just a thug. Most figured he collected for the loan sharks for living, but no one could prove it. Eddie remembered his wife fell from a rooftop garden watering plants.

"As far as I know," Eddie said, "Pitlor and Mac disappeared. Salvi ended up in the marsh a couple of years ago. The other two, the latest ones, we know where they are."

"Both of them, or all of them, with you in the shadow," Dana said.

"No shit. Someone looks at this, they figure me before and after Cronus. A real closet marsh psycho."

"Then why would Preston tell you he's done with you, with Fisher?"

"Maybe he hopes I relax, fuck up, make a mistake."

"Or maybe he believes it isn't you?"

"Would you if you were him?" Eddie asked. "And what about Gwen? If she was involved somehow, then was she playing me, even through the whole Cronus thing."

Eddie took a long pull on his beer.

Dana looked back at him. He didn't need to say what they were both thinking.

"And that's not the end of it," Eddie said. "The last one, Kyle Hardy, if it's who I think it is, he was the guy I killed, the missing body."

Dana shook his head. "What?"

"I remembered the night of the accident with Gwen, a picture they passed out at a rape scene a year before. I was there looking around the marsh behind Oak Island. I think I saw him, the rapist. The face was the same."

"The same as what?

"The Cronus murderer."

"Fucking A...You mean you killed a guy on this list?" Dana tapped the list with his finger.

"Bingo...I just killed him ten minutes too late. And worse, I may have let him go a year or so before that."

They fell silent. Dana slid him another beer.

The familiar guilt hit Eddie in the stomach, as it had over the years, mornings after a drunken blackout, guys at work whispering about him. But this guilt was stronger. This guilt was dangerous, and he knew why.

"I was drunk the night of that rape, so I wandered off on my own, mostly to avoid people. But after I spotted him, I passed out back there, five, maybe ten minutes. I couldn't tell anyone. I was already on thin ice."

"How could you know?" Dana asked.

"That's not the point." Eddie swallowed hard. "I could have stopped it."

The door swung open and two more guys with dirty overalls came in, track workers. They sat on the other side. Dana set two beers down for them, then came back and leaned in front of Eddie. "How did he make the list?" Dana asked, getting back to business. "The rape?"

"The cops knew who it was, but they never found him."

Dana cracked his own beer behind the counter, put it on the bar.

"You ever think of Roman in all this?" Eddie asked.

"How does he figure?"

"Who knows, like you said, the list of people who wanted him dead is too long." He looked once around the bar. "I found some tow slips in his desk. All billed to the police. Not much else. No drugs. It didn't look like he got robbed." He fished in his back pocket, pulled out a slip. "This one, called to Marsh Road a few months ago, RPD, but no name." He handed it over.

Dana looked at it. "Don't you need a name on these to get paid?"

"Unless someone wanted to keep this one off book," Eddie said.

"Then why write it at all?" Dana asked.

"Keep his own record, maybe," Eddie said. He turned his eyes to the list. "This next to the last name. I remember this guy." Eddie pointed to the name *Dennis Morris*. "I had to question him once about a murder, his ex-girlfriend."

"Really?"

"They cut him loose early on, though. He had an alibi."

"Where is he now?"

"Still in the city, I think. Works on the beach." Eddie paused. "He's the only one alive or not missing. I can find him," he said. "The others, I need to know more about these guys. The missing ones would have landed on another desk, not mine."

"Whose?"

"Fisher probably?"

"The recent two," Eddie said, "I was already on the outside."

"So, where do you look?"

"If it's Fisher, probably where the cases went cold. But I don't think the RPD will have an open-door policy for me."

Dana held up a finger. "One minute," he said and walked

away and into the back office. Eddie sipped his beer and looked at the guy sleeping in a booth like he was home taking a nap on the couch. For a second, he was jealous.

When Dana came back, he sat on the stool next to him. "I know somebody who might be able to help."

"Who?"

"He owes me," Dana said.

Eddie backed off the question. He knew Dana had his lists, too, and they were for his eyes only.

"What's this going to cost me?" Eddie asked.

"Don't worry," Dana said. "I'm keeping a tab."

Eddie welcomed the joke. It temporarily masked the pain of what Gwen may have done to him, maybe the only person he ever really trusted besides Dana. It was hard enough to have to live without her and mourn her death because of his bad judgment, but now, he wasn't even sure he knew the person he was grieving for.

Chapter Fifty-Four

Eddie had another dream. He was at the racetrack in the rain, trying to run through the mud. The horses were a hundred yards in front of him. The more he ran, the more his legs sunk, until he was up to his waste pushing forward, pushing against the sand like cement. He looked to the grandstand, filled with people cheering. Then Gwen was in front of him, walking backward, calling, "come on, Eddie. I can't wait." She was naked and dragging two men by their arms.

"Come on, Eddie." She laughed, and the men laughed, and the mud got deeper, up to his chest, and the crowd laughed, and the horses rounded the turn laughing, and some were behind him, he could hear them coming, the hooves beating. Gwen stopped and looked past him at the two men face down in the mud. Suddenly she couldn't move, her wheelchair was stuck. "Too bad, Eddie."

The rain gathered around him, and soon he was swimming beneath the brown water, beneath the mud, and the horses ran overhead, a thunderous posse.

Chapter Fifty-Five

Dana wasn't playing when he told Eddie he knew people. Not just barflies or loan sharks, but people who could make things happen, or better, people who owed him favors. One of those guys was Melvin Gillis, retired Revere Police. He had been friends with Fisher. They split the duty on the cold cases for a while.

He still had all his hair, gray and long to his shoulders in a ponytail. If you didn't know he was a cop, you would have thought he was a biker come down from Laconia, New Hampshire for someone's funeral.

"Mr. Gillis," Dana said when he walked up to the bar and took a stool. They shook hands.

"How the fuck are you, Dana?"

He held out both hands to the walls, palms up. "With all this, how can I be bad?"

"You love it that much?"

"Enough," Dana said. "What's your call?"

"Anything on draft?"

Dana drew a beer from the tap.

"Why so urgent?" Gillis said. "Today's my golf day."

"The way you hit em, I'm doing you a favor." Dana put the draft down. "Friend of mine is looking for a little news from the old days."

"How old?"

"The last few years in the cold room."

Gillis finished the glass, slid it towards the edge. "Loosen me up," he said. He looked around the empty bar. "How do you make a living in this shit hole?"

"It's early. They'll be in."

Dana returned with a refill, poured himself a cranberry.

"What's this friend want with that kind of news?"

"He's curious."

"So am I," Gillis said.

Dana sipped his juice. He could feel a little heat under his collar. "Let's just say I'd appreciate whatever help you gave us."

"Us?"

"I'm sort of helping him out."

"And how much would it be appreciated?"

Dana leaned in and lowered his voice. "I won't tell your wife you fucked a waitress in my office," he said and dumped the ice from his drink into the sink beneath him.

"She wouldn't believe you anyway." Gillis laughed. Dana reached under the counter and slid a photograph next to his beer. "Think she'd believe this?"

The photo had Gillis with his shirt off behind a woman with exposed breasts. He got quiet; then his face turned sour. "You snuck in and took this, pervert?" he asked.

"You posed for it, you drunk," Dana said.

Gillis grabbed it and ripped it in half, then again, then threw it in the air like confetti.

Dana reached underneath the bar and slid him another one. The same shot. "We can play all day," he said. He knew the last thing Gillis wanted to do was part with a piece of his retirement.

He got quiet for a second. "Okay...what?"

"In the end, the cases that went cold, who pushed for them to stay that way."

Gillis leaned in like he wanted no one else to hear even though the bar was empty. "Anything I tell you, you didn't get it here," he said.

"I never heard it."

"Preston. Sort of."

"Preston?"

"He pushed for a few of them to close. 'Said why waste resources to look for scum, dead or alive.'" Gillis finished his beer. "I guess he figured if they were missing, best to let them stay that way."

161

Dana slid him the list Eddie left.

"Are these the cases he pushed for?" Dana asked.

Gillis read the list in a whisper. "Bill Mac, Pitlor, Salvi," then said, "Could be. The first few I remember, I think. I don't know the last three."

"Two of them have been in the paper not that long ago."

"I don't read it," he said.

Dana filled the draft and put two shots glasses on the bar.

"I didn't get it first hand from Preston, though," Gillis said, as if he suddenly remembered.

"What do you mean?" Dana held a whiskey bottle in his hand.

"It always came from Fisher. Maybe he was driving it himself or with someone else's advice. I couldn't be sure."

Dana poured two whiskeys as the door opened and the preacher with the twelve-inch cross stuck his head in. "Bar's open, father," Dana said, then turned to Gillis and held up the shot. "Up your alley." They threw them back. "Now, the list. What else can you tell me about these guys?"

"Who's the nut?" Gillis asked, looking at the preacher.

"House Chaplin," Dana said, then tapped the bar. "The list?"

Gillis stared at it again, then lifted his head. "That girl in the picture you got," he said to Dana, "is she still around?"

162

Chapter Fifty-Six
The Beast

It's like that song, Kyle thought. the one my old man used to listen to on the porch drinking his beer, 'ever since that night, we've been together.' He hummed it, thought of Gina's limp body beneath him, barely breathing back into his cheek. And the others, falling lifeless in his hands. He stood in the rain, the wild weeds surrounding him, and followed her, watching her move. He was the beast in the jungle now. At home. He made a slight noise, saw her react, changed his voice. She stopped. "Hey," she said, staring into the marsh, the hunted prey, the trophy waiting for his mantel.

Chapter Fifty-Seven

Eddie hit the beach again, the third time this week. He watched a truck from the city move slowly along the sidewalk, four or five guys raking papers and beyond them, a few tractors dragging screens in the sand, cleaning up the seaweed that floated in from Boston Harbor. He walked to Revere Street and back. The air was brisk, the sun playing in and out of the clouds. His steps were longer today, more force, and still no cane.

Afterward, sitting in his car in the driveway listening to a Beatles Song, *Happiness Is a Warm Gun,* he realized he'd worked up a pretty good sweat, the familiar athletic soreness in his calves and thighs reminding him of the days when he'd play basketball for four hours on a Saturday morning. It felt good taking his stiff legs up the short stairs to his apartment, but just before going in, he stopped.

The door was ajar.

He moved instinctively to the side, pushed the door open with one hand and took a slow step inside, then heard a crash, followed by a loud cry. "Fuck!"

When he turned the corner into the kitchen, his adrenaline pumping, he saw Dana standing over a broken mug on the floor. "Fucking handle fell off in my hand," he said.

Eddie looked from his face to the floor. "What the fuck? How did you get in?"

"It was open," Dana said.

"No, it wasn't."

"Okay. I jimmied it." He leaned over and picked up some of the broken pieces. "I had to piss," he said.

Eddie tossed a towel on the floor over the spill, slid the whole thing to the corner with his foot.

"I don't know what's worse," Eddie said, "the nightmare I had last night or your ugly puss sneaking around my kitchen?"

"I'm here on a mission, my friend."

"Really?" Eddie said, and looked at him like he had no idea what he was talking about.

"You *are* still a fucking cop, aren't you?"

"No."

"Up here." Dana pointed to his head and handed him a cup of coffee. "Preston," he said.

Eddie swallowed hard. "What?"

"That's what the guy told me."

"Preston what?" Eddie asked, pacing slowly with his cup.

"Turned those cases cold before their time, at least that's what Fisher was preaching."

He looked at him in disbelief.

"I had pictures, Eddie," Dana said. "Trust me, that cheap prick does not want to give his wife half of anything."

They moved to the living room and sat down. Eddie lit a cigarette. Dana grabbed the pack and joined him.

"What about the list?"

He pulled out a piece of paper and read from it. "Two out of the first three disappeared within six months of each other. Both Tommy Mac and Pitlor left it all behind, bank accounts, clothes, cars. Salvi, they found in the marsh, you must remember that.

"I wasn't on it, but the word was the mob dragged him to the mud," he said. "Bad debts."

"Convenient," Dana said. "Mac had three other battery charges all dropped, Pitlor twice went to trial for rape, once found innocent, once a mistrial. Salvi? Witnesses said he was arguing with his wife, threatening her before she took a dive from the third floor. The others, Cory you know, Bankia too. Bad guys, abusers."

"Fuck," Eddie said. "Some warped justice? And the last ones in the marsh. They had me."

"You?"

"Look where it all headed after. Right up my ass."

Dana dragged deep on the end of the butt and put it out in the ashtray. "Why make it you?

"Better me than them."

"You were a diversion?"

"The timing. Cronus. Too good to pass up."

"Why not just keep it clean, let the scum disappear like the first two."

"Not enough, maybe," Eddie said.

"Enough for what."

"Maybe they needed a marker for the next guy."

"Why?" Dana asked.

"I don't know. Why did warriors take scalps?" When he said it, he said it almost to himself as if it all came clear, right there in the living room, all of it played out in front of him. "To scare them, right?"

"That's fucked up," Dana said, "even for the beach."

"Did he say Preston was telling Fisher what to do?" Eddie asked.

"He wasn't sure who was working who."

"Let's suppose the other way around. Fisher convinces Preston that these guys weren't worth the time, which I agree they weren't, and once the cases got filed down to him in ghostland, they lay there dead."

"No news is good news," Dana said.

Eddie got up, paced around the living room, smoking. "But Roman, that was different."

"More personal?" Dana asked.

Eddie froze for a second like he had a notion he was afraid to entertain.

"And Kyle Hardy?"

"Never closed as far as he knew," Dana said.

"I know it's open now. Preston told me so himself."

The two men stared at each other.

"What are you thinking, Detective?" Dana asked.

"I'm thinking if it was Fisher pulling the strings, who was working him?" He snubbed the butt. "The next to the last name, Morris. I need to see him." He looked at Dana. "Then we need to visit an old friend."

Chapter Fifty-Eight

Eddie liked the way the guy washed the windows. He'd seen him on the beach for fifteen years, tall and hunched, always wore a knit hat rolled at the edges. Everything about him took its time. He couldn't remember if he'd ever heard him talk, but the guy was a staple on the boulevard, and Eddie liked the way he worked, the smooth, effortless stroke with the blade, the way he made each window better in a matter of seconds, each slow swipe over the glass. In a way, he envied him, even if the guy rented a weekly on Shirley Ave, or lived in a box under the bridge. He envied the simplicity of his life, make some money, spend it, wash some more windows. Zen-like.

From his seat on the sea wall across from Mickey's Eddie kept an eye out. It was four in the afternoon, probably the end of his window washing shift, the time when he would disappear into the fading light of the beach, make way for the other crowd: the bankers who went home and traded their Porsches for a Harley, the school teachers from different cities dressing down at night, the tough guys and girls ready for it on every corner.

Eddie and Dana had talked well past midnight. Eddie felt right about Dana being there to help him. Between the two of them, they arrived at a place that made sense. The picture that developed was still a bit blurry, but they agreed on what should happen next.

Not long after Eddie's third cigarette, Dennis Morris walked down the boulevard to the bar, shaking the flour off his shoes on the way. You could tell the guys who fried the food on the beach, they walked a few yards then stamped their feet, then walked again, like the flour had to come off in stages no matter how many times they hit it with the broom.

Someone from inside the bar yelled "goal" when the door opened, and Eddie thought back to Bobby Orr flying through the air against the St. Louis Blues, his one fond hockey memory and probably the last hockey game he watched.

He looked up and down the boulevard, and thought about Preston and their last conversation. In a way, he had let Eddie go that day on the beach, like a father sending his son off to college with nothing but his blessing. Who knows how long it would last, but, for now, Eddie was willing to admit that they'd both been through enough. And in a few days, they would talk again and maybe agree to put it all behind them for good.

He flicked his cigarette on the cold sand and walked across the street to have a drink with Dennis Morris and do the first of a few things he needed to do to make it right.

Chapter Fifty-Nine
The Beast

Cold and frightened, she only fought in the beginning, until the first one dug in. Soon she relaxed in his arms, limp like that first night he felt the power. Then the heat tore at his chest, the voice yelling at him through the rain, the water surrounding him, taking him, his feet along the marsh floor, the slick sand in his fingers, moving past the bodies hiding beneath him, the other marsh souls dragging him along, welcoming him home, to the deep, to the cold, to the river running through his veins, and the moon disappearing behind the clouds.

Chapter Sixty

Ron Fisher lived on a quiet street in Swampscott, the next town over from Lynn. The Lynn beach and the Swampscott beach shared the same four-mile ocean front, the same view of the Boston skyline, but that was about all these two places had in common. Folks from Revere and Lynn saw Swampscott as posh and snobby, a much wealthier town.

Ron's townhouse was a few blocks from the beach.

Eddie and Dana sat in the gold Caddie on the end of the tree-lined street. "Number thirty-eight," Eddie said. "You go around back."

"Will do, Captain." Dana pulled a small silver, two-shot derringer from his pocket, tucked it in the front of his pants.

"Does that thing actually shoot bullets?" Eddie asked.

"Worked the last time I used it," Dana said.

"You should try something more your size." He flipped his leather jacket open to reveal the handle of a police issue six-shot revolver.

"They let you keep that?" Dana asked.

"Not really," Eddie said.

They walked to the front of the townhouse, the sun just peeking up over the ocean nearby, past a few manicured lawns and sidewalk maples. The split was white clapboard, a small front porch on either side with matching blue rocking chairs—*everything in order*. Dana moved down the alley to the back of the yard.

Eddie knocked, made himself visible in the spyglass. No answer. He tried again, then heard some noise inside. When the door opened, Dana was standing behind Ron; the small gun pointed at his back. Eddie pushed the door wide, reached for his gun with his other hand.

"Detective," Dana said.

The three of them moved into the living room, all beige and cloth, some ugly faux-modern print on the wall, the kitchenette a gaudy blue and white. Dana pushed Ron to the couch, made him sit. "Is this how you get even?" Ron asked.

"No, no, I'm over that," Eddie said. He held the gun in his right hand, let it point to the floor. "You've been a bad boy, Ronnie, for a long time." He pulled out the list and read from it. "Tommy Mac, Salvi, Pitlor, Bankia, Cory, ringing any bells?"

Ron looked at Dana, then back to Eddie. "Where'd you get the beef?"

"He came with a coupon," Eddie said. "The names. Recognize them?"

"Why should I?"

"Because you killed some of them."

"I don't know what the fuck you're talking about."

"That's funny," Eddie said. "Dana, is that what you heard?"

"Melvin Gillis," Dana said. "He told me Officer Fisher liked to bury cases in the cold room."

"Fuck him. He's a drunk."

"The same cases as these?" Eddie asked, holding up the list.

"Now that you mention it, there are some names that match," Dana said, in his own rehearsed cop voice.

"What now? Cronus rides again?" Ron asked. "Drag me to the marsh like the others."

"That would be too easy," Eddie said. "I have other plans."

Ron fell silent for a moment then shifted on the couch.

"How many did you kill?" Eddie asked.

"What the fuck are you talking about?"

"Or was it Preston?" *Time to go fishing.*

"Preston?" Ron said. "You're nuts."

Eddie pointed to the list. "All cases under yours and Preston's watch. All of them dead or still missing. All of them abusers who got off. Maybe I'll ask Preston about it myself. Bring us all in for a tea party."

171

Ron let out a laugh looking at the list. "You think Preston whacked them all. How'd you ever make Detective?"

"All? Aren't some of them still missing?" The room got quiet. "Then who?" Eddie asked.

Ron looked from wall to wall, then, back and forth to Eddie and Dana. "I need to know where this is going?" he said.

"It's going where I want it to go. Your only option is telling me the truth, and *maybe* there's a slight chance you walk."

Ron fell silent again.

"Look," Eddie said, "I know the people on that list were scum. And whatever happened to them, they probably deserved. But I need to know everything or I'm walking this into Preston's office."

"He probably wouldn't recognize it if you did," Ron said. "He's not one of us."

Eddie let it go. "You want to take that chance?"

Dana lit a cigarette, threw the match on the floor.

"A Russian, contract guy," Ron said.

"A Pro?" Eddie asked, not really looking for the answer. "Who paid him?"

"The church," Ron answered.

Eddie thought for a second. "The church? About seventy-years-old, glasses, overweight."

"Good guess," Ron said.

Eddie pulled a stool from the nearby kitchenette. He looked at the list again. "Morris was next?"

"On deck," Fisher said.

"And Hardy?"

Fisher smiled. "The rapist. He got off easy. He stayed missing."

"Why him? He didn't slip through the law."

"He was Gwen's pick?"

Eddie felt a burn inside him. Fisher and Gwen working together, Eddie the stooge in the middle. "I don't get it," he said

"The girl he raped; she was messed up after. Gwen tried to

172

help her. She put Hardy on the list. No one argued."

"Why revenge for her?" Eddie asked. "She worked with hundreds of victims."

"Who knows?" Fisher said. "Personal, maybe, or just one too many."

For a second, Fisher felt more human to him. "What about Roman? Why didn't he end up with the others?"

"He got it for a different reason."

"What reason?"

"Gwen."

Eddie knew this already. That night looking through his trailer, then at the burnt tow truck, he felt it, something about it stunk of retribution. He thought of the tow slip he brought home, towing cars for the cops, the one on the Marsh Road a few months ago, and the fact that there were no cars near the murders, except one. Roman was in it somehow; he knew that. Not even the marsh could make these many things disappear without the help of at least one scumbag. Suddenly the room got spinning on him, and for a second, it brought him back there, *the headlights, reaching for Gwen's hand.* He stood and walked it off.

"He claimed he didn't know anyone was there," Fisher said, "that he was just after the car, payback for something."

"You had him hit?" Eddie asked, almost gasping for breath.

"It seemed like the right thing to do. For her," Ron said.

"And me?"

He didn't answer. But Eddie knew already. If he fell that night, it would have been okay. They could have made it look like he'd taken her there, to what? Kill her? Who knows how they would have spun it?

"And me?" Eddie asked again, and then one more time before Ron had a chance to answer, "and me!" He swung his right fist, flush into Ron's face. The contact was swift and true, and it made Ron lean away to the side of the couch, then turn back slowly, working his jaw.

Eddie was staring at him, the gun still hanging by his side, his finger looped in the trigger. He raised it and pointed.

173

Dana stood still. No one spoke. Eddie was working the words around in his head. He wanted to know how Gwen was involved, how she helped to manufacture the list, how she came to work with Stang and Ron, and indirectly, how she helped to murder at least five people. But he couldn't bring himself to do it. He was smart enough to make the connections: Stang with the church, Ron with the department, her with the victims— but right now, standing there, wanting to kill *somebody*, and Ron Fisher being as easy prey as anyone, he couldn't ask the right questions.

He lowered the gun to his side.

"We all have to pay for our sins," he said, "one way or another. I'll give you one chance to make it right or Preston and the papers get everything."

Chapter Sixty-One

A few nights later, Jurek finished the last ounce from a tumbler of martinis. He'd already sat through two private dances and a Cuban cigar. He threw a hundred-dollar bill on the couch before he left, kissed Janice on the cheek, then once on her breast. "For good luck," he said. She giggled, pulled off her blonde wig, shook out her real hair, dark and shoulder length.

He walked from the dressing room through the darkened Surf Club, past the empty tables. It was well after hours, but he was one of the chosen few. He'd come a long way since the early days, even after Dimitri left the country for good, and he had to make his own contacts, often the less glamorous low-life junkyard crowd. But Jurek had managed to make it none the less, girls, money, a condo on the beach. He was living the American dream.

Outside, the wind blew off the beach knocking against the neon sign in the parking lot, the only sound for what seemed like miles. He pulled his black topcoat tight and made his way gingerly across the frost-coated pavement. .

When he unlocked the door to his Mercedes, Ron Fisher walked up to him holding a paper bag.

Jurek turned quickly. His eyes tightened, then he recognized him. "What, no Father Joe?" he said.

"Not tonight," Ron answered and fired one shot from inside the bag, through the chest of Jurek's coat.

Jurek opened his mouth to say something, but Ron fired two more, the same spot and Jurek faded into oblivion.

Ron drove away after, left the dead Russian in the front seat of the car. He thought of Preston's face, what it would look like when the body was discovered in the morning, the same look Preston always had on a crime scene, like *why did I sign up for this*. The image made Ron smile as he turned onto the boulevard, past the newest condo building and the last barroom closing up tight for the night. He'd taken Eddie's deal, what else could he do? It was better than being a cop in jail. The terms were nonnegotiable, the things he had to do, but if it went bad somewhere along the way, he wasn't going down alone. That was for sure. There'd be room on that hellbound bus for everyone.

Chapter Sixty-Two

One week after Eddie and Dana held guns on Ron Fisher in his apartment, Dennis Morris walked out of Mickey's, took a deep breath and mumbled something to himself about starting over, a conversation he'd had many times before. He listened to the muffled music behind him in the bar, a Bob Seager song, *Nutbush City Limits,* put his hands in his pockets, fighting the cold wind that was working down the boulevard.

The Friday night traffic was lighter than usual, the city skyline blinking in the distance, a plane landing over East Boston. It was midnight, and soon the late-night drink crowd would hit the beach for food and fights, looking to vent whatever post-midnight blues they carried.

The beach was like that at night, a dumping ground of irrational emotion, a last chance stage. People did things at night here they never did again, or before. They acted in strange ways, fell under a twilight spell.

Dennis wanted no part of it. He'd seen enough over the years.

He passed by the corner at Revere Street and headed toward his apartment, where he knew he had a six-pack and a bottle of Jack he was hoping to kill. He was off tomorrow, and normally he would make it a late one, probably two movies before he called it quits. He crossed an alley a block from his apartment, heard some men speaking Spanish in the shadow of their stoop across the street.

A car pulled up behind him and slowed to a crawl. He looked once over his shoulder at the headlights blinding him and quickened his pace. The car followed, then pulled ahead of him.

At the next block just before his apartment building, Joe Stang stepped out in front of him. He was holding a gun. "Get in the fucking car," he said.

Dennis looked up the street.

"Now!" Stang said.

Dennis sat silently in the back seat, the gun pointing at him.

"What's this about?" Dennis asked. The driver, Ron Fisher, told him to shut up without turning around.

They pulled onto the circle at the end of Revere Street then onto the Marsh Road. Ron stepped on the gas and the car lurched forward along the empty straight away.

Dennis stared out the window at the cattails blowing in the wind, like he was expecting someone. A storm was coming, and he was fighting the panic rising in his throat. *This wasn't how it was supposed to go.*

They drove past the junkyard, then headed back toward Revere. The road was dark, no headlights in either direction.

Soon after turning around, Dennis heard the tires hit the gravel road. The car slowed to a stop.

Stang stepped from the car. "Get out," he said, holding the back door open and motioning with the gun to the marsh. "That way."

"Hey, this was..." Dennis started.

"Shut up," Ron yelled. "Shut the fuck up!"

Dennis panicked. "What's this all about? Come on, man."

Stang reached out with his other hand and grabbed him by the collar and marched him into the marsh. "This one's for an old friend," he said.

Ron looked over from the driver's side as they disappeared behind the weeds, put a Red Sox cap on his head. A few drops of cold rain fell on the windshield, and he stared through them to the hazy outline of the moon sitting full behind a veil of clouds. He had talked Stang into finishing what they started after the Russian was found dead. Stang liked things finished. Neat. It was an easy sell. He'd always been willing to do what he thought was necessary, like keeping the bodies visible after the first few so that they would be found, send the message to the others thinking about it.

Ron had no choice. Why should they both go down? He never planned on it getting this deep, one, two maybe, real scumbags. At first, it was just information, getting Gwen to back it up, use her sources to get close, keep the cases quiet after, then before he knew it, it went out of control. Stang wanted to cleanse the earth, and Gwen was right there to help him.

He opened the door and followed them into the marsh.

When they got to the river, Stang told Dennis to stop. "Face the highway," he said. Then he felt it— the cold tip against the back of his head.

"Let the kid go," Ron said.

"What the fuck?" Stang said and started to turn around. "Don't move," Ron yelled. "Drop the gun."

Stang dropped his gun to the turf.

"Get the fuck out of here," Ron snapped, and Dennis ran past them to the road, the footsteps disappearing into the distant sound of traffic on the highway.

"Why you?" Stang asked.

"Why not?" Ron said.

Stang took a breath and blessed himself.

Dennis took off up the Marsh Road, the gravel sliding under his feet. A single gunshot rang out, and he slipped in the mud. Dana's Caddie drove up beside him and came to a stop. The door opened, and he jumped in the back seat.

"What the fuck?" Dennis said. "Get out of here."

"Relax," Eddie said. "It's over."

"Too fucking close for comfort," Dennis said and shut the door.

Eddie looked again through the windshield, the rain picking up suddenly, but not really rain, more like ice tapping on the glass. Dana put the wipers on, the streaks like wet ghosts.

"What are we waiting for?" Dennis almost screamed.

"Hold on," Eddie said.

A pair of headlights pulled up behind them.

"Shit," Dennis whispered.

Eddie looked in the rearview mirror. "One minute," he said and stepped out.

Dennis slumped down on the seat. Dana thought he heard him saying a prayer.

Al Preston jumped out from the cruiser that was parked on Dana's bumper. Eddie was expecting him.

"That way," Eddie said. "My guess is he'll take the easy way out."

"Back up is coming," Preston said, the wet drops streaking on his skin. He walked past Eddie with a purpose, his gun already in his hand then shifted gears. Eddie watched his long strides move quickly into the darkness like he was chasing a quarterback on the run.

Eddie opened the Caddie door and got in. "Let's go," he said to Dana, and they pulled off the shoulder and drove straight along the dark Marsh road, the cold rain falling steadily around them.

Chapter Sixty-Three

When Preston walked into the heart of the marsh, Ron Fisher was on one knee next to the body of Joe Stang. He had dragged him partially into the dirty river, like the others. Preston watched him for a few seconds, kept quiet, and pointed his weapon.

When Ron turned, he looked surprised, then quickly smiled, like the little boy caught stealing his father's quarters from the dresser. He stood up, still holding his gun by his side.

Preston kept his aim. "You want to let that drop right there, Ron," he said. "It's over."

Ron laughed. "I should have known," he said, "that fucking Devlin would flip me."

They could hear the sirens in the distance, faint but getting closer. "They'll be here soon," Preston said. "You know what that means."

"Let me guess," Ron said. "Just doing your job, right?" He swayed a little with the cattails behind him, the rain dripping off the lid of his hat. "So, who gets to be the hero?" he asked.

"Nobody," Preston said. "Too much damage."

The sirens were closer now, a few cars just hitting the Marsh Road.

"Do I have a choice?" Ron asked.

Preston didn't answer, just stood staring in the rain.

"Fuck," Ron said. "At least you'll have to live with it. Right, Lieutenant?" He turned toward the highway, tucked his gun under his chin and fired once toward the dark, wet sky.

Chapter Sixty-Four

Two days later, Eddie and Dennis Morris walked into Dana's place at eleven o'clock in the morning. They each took a stool, and Dana pushed two beers in their direction. He reached underneath him and scooped a bowl full of pretzels from a box and put it on the bar.

"You okay?" Dana asked Dennis.

"I'm better," he said. "That was fucked up. I stayed locked in my apartment."

"You did the right thing," Eddie told him. "I'm sorry how it played out. You were never in danger; it just had to seem that way."

"If you say so," Dennis said, and drank half his beer.

Dana put a shot glass down on the bar, filled it with Schnapps.

"What happened to that cop?" Dennis asked.

"He'll get what's coming to him," Eddie said and pulled an envelope from beneath his sweatshirt. "I want you to have this...a little something for your effort."

Dennis looked inside it and ran his thumb over a stack of bills. "Damn," he whispered.

"The church took up a collection," Dana said.

Dennis looked at the envelope again. "I'm not the church-going type."

"Maybe someday," Dana told him.

Eddie lit a cigarette, reached over, pulled another beer from the ice, and put it next to Dennis. "You're good now. All you have to do is forget. Maybe start over somewhere else."

Dennis nodded. "Ya. A change of scenery might be good."

"I know a little place in Florida, used to be my father's,"

Eddie said. "I could set you up for a few months until you got settled."

"Florida? Sounds good. Fuck the snow, right?" He sipped his beer. "Maybe in a few months."

"I was thinking sooner," Dana said and slid the shot glass closer to him.

"Like when?"

"Like tonight," Eddie said and passed him a second envelope. "There's a one-way ticket in there. After you land, take a cab to the condo address written down inside. The key is in there too, and few names of restaurants might be looking for help."

Dennis picked up the shot glass and threw it back, then looked at them, first one then the other. "Do I have a say in this?"

"We recommend it," Dana said. "It's the best thing for everybody. You don't want cops asking you any more questions, do you?"

Eddie put a hand on his shoulder. "Look at it as an opportunity to put Revere Beach behind you. Nothing but trouble here, anyway."

Dennis finished his beer, took a breath. "Maybe you're right."

Dana filled the shot glass again.

Dennis threw it back. "I guess I should say thanks."

"No need," Eddie said. "Just leave the key under the mat in three months."

Dana put three more beers on the bar. "I love happy endings."

Chapter Sixty-Five

The rest of the Calvary showed up to find Stang and Fisher side by side in the marsh that night, their bodies half out of the stink. Preston filed his story, the anonymous phone call that led him there, and how he found them both dead. The investigation would become involved, with all that went on before it, but in the end, Stang would be buried at St. Rose, all the drunks he helped in attendance. "A sober Irish wake," Eddie mused later, reading the obit in the paper.

Stang would get the proper treatment as a victim of a homicide, and Ron as a suicide, but the record would show they had conspired to murder five men, accused but not convicted of battery and abuse on women they knew. To some people that made them heroes, to others, it made them no better than the people they killed. Who's to say they weren't doing the Lord's work, Eddie thought one morning sipping the last drop of homemade coffee. After all, he had crossed a name off the list himself.

Gwen's name never came up in the investigation. That was part of the deal with Preston, and it left Eddie to remember her as the angel who helped him chase demons from his soul, even if she couldn't chase them from her own. He knew getting Gwen right in his mind would take him a long while, but for now, he was hanging onto the person who shared his love for movies, home-cooked meals, and any kind of jazz with a horn.

"Maybe they're all the lucky ones," he whispered to himself, staring out the window at the empty street. He wasn't sure what he believed as far as life after death went, but he knew what he was afraid of, that big trial court in the sky. He wanted to believe that Gwen was at peace, not having to live with the mistakes she made or the abuses she suffered in this life. And who knows, he thought, maybe she got to visit the Cronus murderer in hell and beat him with a stick every day just for kicks.

Chapter Sixty-Six

Eddie and Dana walked to the racetrack entrance a few weeks after it all got sorted out. Slight snow was falling from the gray afternoon sky. Eddie's stride was stronger, the cane now leaning against his kitchen wall back home like some antique he inherited from his grandfather.

They walked through the half-full parking lot, like kids going to a carnival.

"So," Dana said, "Fisher never got a conscience all those years?"

"I doubt it," Eddie said.

"And Preston never told you how it played out?" Dana asked.

"Some secrets belong to the marsh, right?"

"Smug prick," Dana said. "You're as bad as they are."

"Not quite," Eddie answered.

Dana smiled. "We did alright working together, didn't we Detective?"

"Maybe there's a future in it," Eddie said and reached into his pocket and paid the man in the booth for two entries to the clubhouse.

"The kid, Morris. Why only three months in the condo?" Dana asked. "You planning something after that?"

"I don't know. Maybe I'll make a move myself," Eddie said. "Go south and start a rib joint or something."

"You? A restaurant? You'll need someone who knows the business."

"Know anyone?" Eddie asked.

Dana laughed. "Maybe," he said. "But it'll cost you. No one works for free anymore."

"The first one is on me," Eddie said.

"About fucking time," Dana said, walking into the crowded clubhouse lobby. "Top shelf," he yelled to the bartender. "And make it a double."

Chapter Sixty-Seven

Eddie stopped going to the marsh. Once in a while, he'd cruise by slow, maybe at night, on his way back from the races. But he didn't pull over, didn't get out like before. He was happy to use the road as they intended it, a way to get from here to there.

This particular morning he drove by early, the sun was shining, a few white egrets were flying low looking for silverfish or baby snappers. The breeze was slight, and the weeds danced a silent dance as if they were waving goodbye to the passing traffic.

He thought about the things that were behind him but not forgotten, the mistakes, the guilt over Gwen's death, not being sober enough to stop the beast (if it was him), and the pain of not being sure. He knew that he would have to live with these things, the best way he knew how, for a long time to come. But he was confident he could do that. When it came to living with guilt, God knows he had a lot of practice.

He passed the junkyard, saw the open gates and a few bikers on Harleys hanging by the trailer. New owners, he thought. Some things never change.

At the next intersection, he turned left and followed the beach to Broadway, then into Chelsea, where he drove for ten minutes and pulled over in front of St. Rose Church. The guy on the phone had told him the open meeting started at 9:00 sharp. Eddie rolled down the window, lit a cigarette, and sat in the car watching people descending the basement stairs in groups of two or three. They looked happy. He thought about his father for a second, and his mother, the shit he put them through. He thought about Gwen and what might have been.

He flicked the butt onto the street and rolled up the

window. "Not today," he said to himself and drove back toward Revere to walk the beach before lunch.

Chapter Sixty-Eight
The Beast

The following summer there was a drought. The city imposed a water ban for three months, no sprinklers, no watering plants, no washing cars. It was so dry the surface water in the marsh began to disappear. The levels hit record lows by September. Much of the plant life in the inner marsh was showing roots. Mudflats were popping up from beneath their normal wet cover, and the banks of the river were showing red feet of clay that baked in the late summer sun.

On the far end of the marsh where the water level dropped particularly low was a rivulet passing just to the side of Dizzy Bridge. It worked its way into the brush, emptying into a shallow pool beneath a long thicket of thorn and berry bushes. The only way to get near it was maybe by canoe in a record flood.

At the back of this pool, through the zigzag of branches and weeds, was the shape of a decomposed human hand, peeking out of the water. A red flannel shirt was floating next to it, moving back and forth slightly with the wind. The shirt looked like it would have floated away if not for the spray of reeds growing up through the handful of holes in the chest.

Fantastic Books
Great Authors

darkstroke is
an imprint of
Crooked Cat Books

- Gripping Thrillers
- Cosy Mysteries
- Romantic Chick-Lit
- Fascinating Historicals
- Exciting Fantasy
- Young Adult
- Non-Fiction

Discover us online
www.darkstroke.com

Find us on instagram:
www.instagram.com/darkstrokebooks

Made in the USA
Monee, IL
14 December 2021

85405903R00108